A SCAR
IS BORNE

Dire McCain

APOPHENIA

This book is a work of fiction. The names, characters, and incidents are products of the author's vivid and arguably deranged imagination or have been used fictitiously. Any resemblance to real persons, living or dead, or events is in all probability coincidental. It should be obvious, but lest it not be, the characters' views and beliefs, some of which are psychopathic, are not representative of the author's.

Cover illustration by Sean Madden. To purchase prints, or other drawings and paintings by the artist, please visit his website: seanmaddenart.com

Cover design by Díre McCain

Previous and incomplete versions of the following stories originally appeared elsewhere:

"Papanicolaou Test: A Grand Guignol" in *Clinical, Brutal… An Anthology Of Writing With Guts*, "Cura Te Ipsum" in *Clinical, Brutal 2: Incisive Writing With Guts*, "Procedure 769: CDC# B66883" in *A Dream Of Stone: And Other Ghost Stories*, "Myiagros" in *Dead Sheep*

For you, whoever you are...

PAPANICOLAOU TEST: A GRAND GUIGNOL

CHARACTERS

Uxor
Dr. Art(thur) Sterben, Ob/Gyn
Rudolf Virchow

SETTING

Newport Beach, California, United States of America

Biological Clock

Noun

1) The period of time from puberty to menopause, marking a woman's ability to bear children.

2) The defective gene that drives a woman to blindly obsess over procreating by a certain age, regardless of whether she's fit to be a mother.

1

"Gimme that *People* magazine, Arthur."

Every time you call me Arthur I want to belt you across the face and fracture your mandible, so you will desist once and for all. It is Art, not Arthur. It has always been Art, but the instant I acquiesced to your incessant hounding and placed that three-carat diamond on your digitus annularis, it became Arthur. It drives me out of my fucking mind, and you refuse to stop, no matter how many times I have begged.

"The one with Oprah on the cover. Here, gimme it."

Ah yes, your idol and guru, even though you are a flagrant racist, who comes from a long line of flagrant racists. How on earth would you function without her? Heaven forbid if you had to form your own opinions and make decisions for yourself. If that egomaniacal brainwasher commanded you to spread feces all over your face, like cold cream, and go out in public, you would do it, you obtuse cunt.

Art(hur) picks up the magazine from the coffee table and hands it to his wife.

"Woah! Doesn't Angelina Jolie look super hot? I can't believe she just had twins!"

The inspiration behind that banal, gaudy coccyx tattoo, to which you so proudly draw attention at every opportunity. Also responsible for your ostensible and arrantly hypocritical fascination with sapphism. It is common knowledge that you are the worst homophobe who has ever walked the face of the earth, but now that it is chic to be a pseudo-lesbian, you love dykes, except for my sister Naomi, who is a real lesbian. You treat your annoying yippy dog's vomit with more respect.

"Don't forget, we have to be at the Jones' in an hour."

How could I possibly forget, you insufferable nag? You have only been reminding me every other minute since I crawled back into this self-imposed prison from my exhausting job, which eats hours of my life, all so you can squander the lion's share of my arduously earned dollars at that extortionate day spa and Fascist Island. If you only knew how much I would delight in chopping off every inch of that garishly streaked hair and yanking out those hideous French-pedicured ungues with a pair of tenaculum forceps. And do not get me started on that god damn wardrobe. There is a plethora of usuriously expensive designer clothing in your closet that you have not worn so much as once, yet you continue to acquire more on a weekly basis.

"Better start getting ready now, Arthur. Just DVR that stupid fight and watch it later. I'll never understand why you like all that violence, anyway."

That is too rich, coming from a woman who has a lengthy history of domestic violence against men. You and your false sense of entitlement. When the queen hydra does not get her way, out come the bloodthirsty claws. I should have heeded Richard's warnings, the lucky bastard. He must be counting his blessings every day since you slid your venomous fangs out of him and dug them into my carotid artery. Of course, you are an abject coward when dealing with members of your own gender, because they may strike back, which would be

3

terrifically just. A fractured nasal bridge and zygomatic bone would be the most effective treatment for your disease, you sadistic bitch. If only I could write a prescription.

"David's super excited to show you the work he had done on the master bathroom. He's totally hip on the latest trends in home décor and interior design. You need to take a lesson from him."

Art(hur) glances up at his wife, who's avidly flipping through the pabulumzine, naively swallowing every contrived word and image, as though it were gospel. He lets out a cough of disgust, then picks up his coffee mug, takes a swig, and places it back on the coaster.

David is a pompous, mind-numbingly boring dick. I hate the son of a bitch. I have nothing in common with him, but since his uptight whore of a wife is your best friend, I am forced to act as though I like the patrician bastard and that I give a flying fuck about his god damn renovations. Him and his daddy's easy money. Of course he is hip on the latest trends, because he has no idea what it is like to be forced to work for a living. Neither do you. I knew marrying you was a monumental mistake. It serves me right for seeing dollar signs and erroneously believing I would be sitting on easy street if I took the plunge. I should have known your father was a fucking miser when he refused to pick up the check the night I met him. Oh god, what I would give to be able to go back and know what I know now.

"Okay, Arthur, are you listening to me?"

I cannot help but listen to you, because your voice sounds like a god damn magpie, cawing incessantly. Try as I may, I can never tune you out. Even when you are on the opposite side of the world, I can still feel that agonizingly shrill voice reverberating in my primary auditory cortex. Caw, caw, caw, caw, caw, caw, caw, caw, caw, caw!

"Because I have something super important to tell you. I was gonna wait until tomorrow night, when we have dinner with Dad, but the excitement is killing me!"

Oh no, here we go again. I wonder how much it is going to set me back this time, you useless parasite.

"It's super exciting! Here, put this back."

Art(hur) takes the magazine from his wife's hand and places it on the coffee table.

I am certain it is just thrilling, I am on the edge of my seat, and of course, it cannot wait until this round is over. You must tell me right this instant, mustn't you?

"Are you ready?"

I will never be ready, interested, or receptive, but you will tell me regardless.

"I'm pregnant!"

> Marriages are not normally made to avoid having children.

Art(hur) looks up at his wife, visibly stunned.

Jesus fucking Christ! No! No! No! Those words did not just pour out of your rima oris!

"Did you hear me, Arthur? I said, I'm pregnant! Isn't that, like, the most super thing you've ever heard?"

Art(hur)'s gape turns into a blank stare.

> If the man of science chose to follow the example of historians and pulpit-orators, and to obscure strange and peculiar phenomena by employing a hollow pomp of big and sounding words, this would be his opportunity, for we have approached one of the greatest mysteries which surround the problem of animated nature and distinguish it above all other problems of science. To discover the relations of man and woman to the egg-cell would be almost equivalent of the egg-cell in the body of the mother, the transfer to it by means of the seed, of the physical and mental characteristics of the father, affect all the questions which the human mind has ever raised in regard to existence.

You scheming cunt! This was all planned! Oh god, why did I consent to fucking you that night? You repulse me, you adulterous whore! It was a god damn miracle I was able to achieve an erection in the first place, never mind maintain it, while sloshing about in that maculate, cavernous vagina of yours! I should have known you were lying about taking the Tri-Cyclen! You were probably taking Clomid instead!

And I bet it was my bitch partner who gave it to you! God damn you, both! I made it abundantly clear at the outset of this intolerable misalliance that I did not want any children! Have you no mercy at all? How in god's name can you even consider dragging an innocent child into this multi-car train wreck with you in the conductor's seat?

"Aren't you gonna say anything, Arthur?"

Art(hur) remains silent, his eyes now affixed on the cartoonishly airbrushed portrait of his wife hanging over the fireplace.

"I hate you! You're totally impossible! I'm having this baby, with or without your blessings! Who cares what you think, anyway! You have no say! It's *my* body!"

> Only those who regard healing as the ultimate goal of their efforts can, therefore, be designated as physicians.

Without saying a single word, Art(hur) goes into the bedroom and retrieves the loaded Smith & Wesson Model 500 from the sock drawer. Returning to the living room, he grabs his wife by the throat, slams her down on the floor, and pulls up her dress, ignoring her bewildered screams. After ripping off her overpriced size-five Cosabella lace panties – which were already bursting at the seams, struggling to accommodate her size-seven ass – he spreads apart her labia and shoves the barrel up into her cervical canal, like a speculum, then pulls the trigger four times.

Looming over her twitching body, he falls into a state of suspended animation, while pondering whether he should fellate the 8-3/8″ barrel and suck out that last spermatozoon, or shoot it up into the primigravida's lead-filled womb.

Eleven minutes and 23 seconds later, he snaps out of it. Leaving the gun barrel embedded in her warm yet lifeless and prolapsed uterus, he goes into the kitchen, removes a pint of Häagen-Dazs Butter Pecan from the freezer and a tablespoon from the silverware drawer, then returns to the living room to watch the last three rounds of the fight before retiring for the night.

> Disease is not something personal and special, but only a manifestation of life under modified conditions, operating according to the same laws as apply to the living body at all times, from the first moment until death.

> *omnis cellula e cellula*

CURA TE IPSUM

Being a medical examiner was her life's calling and a tremendous source of pride. She had toiled for years putting herself through school, with no support from anyone. *"That's disturbing! That's creepy! That's weird!"* were the inevitable reactions from women whenever she revealed her line of work. They would invariably zero in on the morbidity, refusing to recognize the deeper and more meaningful layers in what was truly a public service.

With the body properly positioned on the stainless steel table, she placed the body block under the back, causing the chest to protrude while the arms and neck fell back, fully exposing the torso.

Women reveled in criticizing every aspect of her life, relentlessly reminding her that she was defective for not having a husband and children. The very idea that it was *her choice* to remain single and childless was beyond their shallow realm of comprehension. Rather than admitting they were narrow-minded, they *blamed her* for not conforming to their spoon-fed ideology.

She picked up the scalpel and slid it into the right shoulder, methodically pulling it across to the xiphoid process. She repeated the action with the left shoulder then pulled the scalpel from the sternum down to the pubis, deviating to the left of the umbilicus, ensuring that the incision was deep enough to reach the rib cage and abdominal wall. The body began to hemorrhage.

She thought "misogyny" was among the most misused and overused words in the English language. Men had always treated her with respect and equality. She never understood why women were incessantly whining about sexism, which she saw as a cop-out. It had never held her back. Women were irreproachable martyrs who imputed their own incompetence to male chauvinism. The way she saw it, if one behaved as an equal, one would be treated as such. Acknowledging, not to mention obsessing over, ostensible differences only made them real.

She peeled back the skin, muscle, and soft tissues from the thoracic wall, then placed the scalpel on the instrument tray. Then she pulled the top flap over the face, exposing the front of the rib cage and infrahyoid muscles in the front of the neck. The body continued to bleed out.

She only enjoyed the company of women when they were lying lifeless on her autopsy table. Men were nowhere near perfect, especially when they allowed their dicks to guide them, but she would always feel more at ease with them than she would ever feel with women. Far too many lunches and happy hours with her male colleagues were ruined by the presence of women, even one. They would bitch and moan no end, and knock whatever they didn't understand, expecting her to take their side, simply because she too had two X chromosomes. She would have changed that at the first opportunity, if it were possible.

She picked up the shears and cut through the ribs on the sides of the thoracic cavity. When finished, she placed the shears on the tray, picked up the scalpel, and began pulling off the chest plate, while removing the posteriorly attached soft tissues. With the final tug, she noticed the heart was still beating, albeit slowly. The blood was now clouding her visibility. She placed the scalpel on the tray and picked up the hose, then washed the blood down the drain as it poured out.

Being trapped among a pack of women was sheer torture. The most violative social occasions by far were the wedding showers, baby showers, and bachelorette parties she had been forced to attend to earn pay raises and promotions at work. Vacuous bitchfests disguised as female bonding sessions that would obliterate her self-respect, causing her to feel ashamed for days, as if she had prostituted herself.

After restoring adequate visibility, she placed the hose on its holder and picked up the scalpel, using it to cut open the pericardial sac. When finished, she cut the abdominal muscle away from the bottom of the rib cage and diaphragm, exposing the organs beneath. A faint gurgling sound came out of the body's mouth, as the heart stopped beating.

"Sisterhood" was a fallacy. Women existed solely to betray, judge, and instill crippling self-doubt, often in the form of back-handed compliments. They were frighteningly jealous and competitive in the pettiest ways. They were a nightmare to work for, and would always abuse a position of authority. They wouldn't hesitate to lie in order to discredit other women they felt threatened by. They would drop everything and everyone, even their own children, for a man.

The blood continued to flow and was once again clouding her visibility. She placed the scalpel on the tray, then picked up the hose and washed the blood down the drain. After placing the hose on its holder, she picked up the scalpel and cut off the carotid and subclavian arteries, before moving on to the larynx, detaching both it and the esophagus from the pharynx. Then she cut the rest of the chest organs from their attachments at the spine.

Every female she had encountered in her life was the same, beginning with her mother. She would give herself wholly and trust implicitly, only to be crushed by their hormonally-driven cruelty, as if it were their god-given right to misplace their nastiness onto her, simply because she was there and breathing.

She cut the diaphragm away from the body wall and pulled out the abdominal organs, then used the scalpel to separate the organs from their attachments at the pelvic ligaments, bladder, and rectum, freeing them up in one block. Then she placed the scalpel on the tray and pulled out the organs in one fell swoop, gently placing the block on the plastic-covered floor.

Her parents never should have been together, let alone married and had a child. They had only been dating for five months when her actress-cum-stripper mother ensnared her wealthy lawyer father by getting pregnant. Motivated by sloth and greed, her mother knew a child would be her ticket to a steady source of income, without having to work herself. Her father was a noble man, who took full responsibility, despite the oncoming train.

After hosing down the body once more, she slid out the body block from under the back and secured it under the head. Then she picked up the scalpel and began cutting from behind the left ear, over the crown of the head, to behind the right ear, making certain the incision was deep enough to reach the skull. The bleeding resumed, albeit at a trickle's pace.

Her father couldn't have a moment of peace. Her mother would nag him for hours every night when he came home from the office. It was the highlight of her mother's day. Her mother always found a way to ruin his days off as well. The lawn needs mowing, the car needs washing, that hole in the wall needs repairing, etc. Her mother had convinced herself that the poor man was simply sitting around all day, when in truth, he was working himself into a premature grave so his daughter would never have to go without, as he had in his childhood. Then there were the infidelities. Her mother wore the pants while her father wore the horns.

The skin and soft tissues were now divided into two flaps. She placed the scalpel on the tray and began pulling the front flap down over the face to expose the anterior part of the skull. It was requiring more effort than usual, but soon cooperated. Once the front flap was in place, she pulled the back flap down over the nape, exposing the rest of the skull.

During the divorce, her mother had used her as a pawn, going so far as to accuse her father of sexually abusing his own child. Her mother forced her to lie about it, threatening to have her beloved cat, Loki, euthanized if she didn't. She was only five at the time, and incapable of understanding the magnitude of her actions. Even though the allegations were eventually proven false, her father was devastated and would never recover. He died of a broken heart, three days before her seventh birthday. She never forgave herself or her mother.

She picked up the electric saw and began cutting around the cranium, ensuring the incision was deep enough, while being careful not to nick the brain. Then she removed the calvarium and dura mater, exposing the top of the brain. She traded the electric saw for the hose, which she used to wash down the head. Then she placed the hose on its holder, picked up the scalpel, and cut the spinal cord and tentorium cerebella. After placing the scalpel back on the tray, she lifted out the brain and placed it in a prefilled formalin specimen jar. It would be the first in her collection.

She often fantasized about killing her mother, who would have been her first victim, if she were still alive. Self-serving right up until the end, her mother had committed suicide – over a man, no less – by driving her Porsche into a lamppost one night, *after* strapping her ten-year-old daughter into the passenger's seat. Miraculously, the daughter escaped from the crushed car with minimal injuries, moments before it exploded. The vision of her mother flailing and screaming as the flames devoured her was permanently etched into the daughter's young mind. She was not traumatized by the horrific sight of her mother's torturous death, but rather by how close *she* had come to suffering a similar fate at her mother's hands.

Dead, ten times over, the body was ready to be disposed of. She picked up the hacksaw sitting on the floor near the instrument tray and began the lengthy dismemberment process. After reducing the body to several medium-sized chunks, she shoved the pieces into the industrial grinder in the far right corner of the basement. The resultant mincemeat was then dumped into a heavy-duty black garbage bag and dragged out to her two pot-bellied pigs. She watched the sun rise as the beasts slopped down the remains, before returning to the basement, tossing the empty bag in the garbage can on her way in. She lifted her face shield, removed her gloves, and grabbed the bottle of water sitting on the instrument tray. After guzzling all 500 milliliters in one shot, she tossed the empty bottle in the recycling bin. Then she recorded the evening's activities in her logbook. The date was March 8, 2015.

The woman at the night club couldn't have been a more ideal mark. Man-hating and woman-trusting to a fault, she never suspected that a fellow female, a "sister in arms," who had offered such an understanding and agreeable ear, would be capable of such horrors. The stupid, gullible bitch was already plastered when the vapid conversation began, making it a cinch to slip the Flunitrazepam into her Screwdriver undetected. When they rushed out of the place, one of them staggering, people assumed that the barely conscious woman had knocked back five too many. Moments later, she was out cold, oblivious to the hellish fate that awaited her.

Even though the woman was petite, transporting the dead weight from the car to the basement was a strenuous task. She would need to find an easier way, especially if she intended to execute women weighing over 100 pounds, which accounted for most. There's no fudging one's bodyweight in death. After heaving the carcass onto the autopsy table, she administered the Pancuronium Bromide, which ensured full paralysis with sustained sensation. It was mandatory that the woman feel as much pain as possible.

Then came the body block and that first cut.

It's impossible to determine what finally set her off. The compulsion to exterminate had presumably been there all along, tumescing, suppurating. Women were a pestilence that needed to be wiped out. Their congenital inability to control their erratic moods was a plague to society that was rarely spoken about and always forgiven. There was no doubt in her mind that decimating the gender was another public service. She only wished that she could dispose of more than one at a time.

PROCEDURE 769: CDC# B66883

ANALYST: The subject was born prematurely in Fort Bragg, North Carolina, on January 15, 1953, after his alcoholic father had kicked the subject's alcoholic mother in the abdomen with such force she began to hemorrhage. It was an act that would set the precedent for the subject's harrowing childhood, during which he would suffer regular beatings from both parents. The subject was the fifth of nine children.

April 20, 1992 6:40 PM PDT

OPERATOR: "I have a collect call from Robert Alton Harris, an inmate at San Quentin State Prison. Will you accept the charges?"

ROBERT ALTON HARRIS: Eleven whole hours and forty-one minutes. Shoulda been five whole hours and forty-one minutes, but all them people still tryin' to save me are only delayin' my fate. Need someone to claim my remains, that's all, ain't askin' for the world. Been waitin' to die since before I was born. Now, the Grim Reaper's knockin' at my door and nobody'll step

17

up to the plate. Cousin Sam's my last hope, but as soon as he opened his mouth, I knew it was a lost cause. He was fucked up, and I was fucked, destined for Boot Hill, with the likes of Bluebeard Watson and William Kogut, to spend eternity stuck in Hell.

VICTIM: *It was the morning after Fourth of July. My best friend and I were going fishing. We stopped at Jack in the Box to get some breakfast. We were eating in the car when two men walked up.*

> When the subject was nineteen months old, his father flogged him with a bamboo cane, breaking the subject's jaw. It was the first of numerous serious injuries sustained during his childhood.

All these years, everybody thinkin' I wasn't sorry for killin' them two boys, thinkin' I was chickenshit, not wantin' to meet the maker. Hell, I ain't denyin' what I done was wrong, and I come to terms with dyin', but the stories I heard 'bout the hereafter up on that Hill's enough to make the toughest son of a bitch cringe.

One of them had a gun. He told us to let him in the car, so we did. He held the gun at us and said to start driving. He said he wasn't going to hurt us. The other man followed in their car. I didn't know where we were going or why, but I was really scared.

> Even meals in the subject's home were a source of trauma and abuse. While at the dinner table, if the subject reached for anything without his father's permission, the subject's father would

drive a fork through the back of the subject's
hand. The subject would then be forbidden to eat
another bite until he had "learned his lesson,"
often resulting in several days of starvation.

Goddamn story of my life. Ain't had real food since
1978. Now I got one foot in the grave, and here comes
the pizza, the fried chicken, the works. Cigarettes been
like bullion all these years, and now I'm sittin' on a
case. And the new duds. Why the heck they think a
condemned man needs new duds is beyond me. All I
care 'bout's not windin' up on that Hill. They say it's
like Purgatory, only worse, 'cause it ain't temporary,
you're stuck there for all eternity, sufferin' in ways you
ain't never suffered in your worst nightmares.

*When we reached the Lake, the man told us to pull in and
stop the car. Then he told us to get out and start walking. He
followed us with the gun held to our backs. He joked and
laughed a lot, and kept promising he wouldn't hurt us. He
said he just wanted the car and that we'd be free to go. We
believed him and kept walking.*

Recreation was equally abusive and traumatic.
The subject's father's idea of Hide-and-Seek was
to give the subject and his siblings a half-hour to
hide outside, before hunting them down with a
loaded shotgun, threatening to shoot anyone who
was found.

Just after three, new duds on, stomach fulla grease,
lungs fulla nicotine, they come get me, strap me in,
and release the dogs. Ready to roll, even tell 'em so.

Look 'round, see 'em all here watchin', every one of 'em I wronged. No more get outta jail free cards, my number's up. It'd take a goddamn miracle to save me now. Got no choice but to suck it up and take what I got comin' like a man.

"PULL IT."

I heard a loud popping sound. Then I felt a hot burning sensation in my back. A few seconds later, I heard another loud popping sound, and felt another hot burning sensation, but in my head. I fell down. I couldn't see or move. But I could hear. I could hear the man laughing.

A couple of months prior to the subject's tenth birthday, the Harris family relocated to a farm labor camp in the San Joaquin Valley area of California. Soon after, the subject's eldest sister was arrested for theft and sent to juvenile hall, where she revealed yet another form of abuse in the Harris home.

The subject's father habitually molested the subject's sisters, frequently forcing the subject to watch. The subject described one incident in particular when his father tried to force him to take part in the assault. When the subject was unable to achieve an erection – presumably due to the atrocious nature of the situation – he was beaten unconscious and locked in a closet until the following day. In early 1963, the subject's father was deemed a sex offender and sent to Atascadero State Hospital for eighteen months. Upon his release, the molestation resumed until the end of 1964, when he was caught in the act by two police officers who had been dispatched to the Harris home on a domestic violence call. The subject's father was tried and incarcerated for the crimes.

Ten minutes into it, another no go. They cut me loose, and here I am, back in that ol' cell, eatin' jelly beans, smokin' Camels, waitin' to die. Reckon it might never happen, but scared to let my guard down, 'cause in the backa my mind, that Hill's still bellowin' at me, like a lion at feedin' time.

I heard my best friend screaming. It sounded like he was running away. Then I heard two more popping sounds. The man started laughing again. I was never more scared in all my life. I felt the man standing over me. I could hear him breathing. I wanted to get up and run, but I still couldn't see or move. He pushed my body with his foot and asked me if I was dead yet. I wished my dad was there. He would have killed the man and rescued us, I know it.

With the subject's father in prison, the Harris family migrated up and down the valley for a couple of years, following the crops. Then the subject's mother moved the subject and five of his siblings to Sacramento, where she took up with a new man. By now the subject had already had a number of run-ins with the law, including serving four months in juvenile hall for stealing a car. In 1967, the subject's mother abandoned him, claiming he had become impossible to rear. The subject, now fourteen, was left to fend for himself.

They say it's a frozen, pitch-dark wasteland. Can't see a goddamn thing, can't move neither. Like that picture, *Johnny Got His Gun,* 'cept worse, 'cause your smellin' and hearin's stronger than a hound dog's. The stencha death, and your own flesh rottin' away, swallows you whole, and every sound cuts through your ears and into your brain, like an ice pick bein' drove through your head. Worsta all's what's happenin' inside your head. It turns into a big ol' TV, 'cept the only show's your worst pains and traumas. Ain't got no off switch neither, it just keeps on goin' and goin', playin' over and over again.

The man walked away. I heard the car start and burn rubber. The laughing stopped. It was quiet, so quiet it hurt my ears. I was going to die. I thought about Mom and what it would do to her. I wished I'd stayed home that day. I wished I'd stayed home. I. Wished. I'd. Stayed. Home.

> The subject made his way to Oklahoma, where a brother and sister resided. After being kicked out of school, stealing another car, and fleeing to Florida, the subject was arrested and sent to a federal reformatory for the remainder of his adolescence. While there, he was diagnosed as schizophrenic with both suicidal and homicidal tendencies. When the subject reached adulthood, he was released from custody. With fifty dollars in his pocket and a one-way bus ticket, he headed to Chula Vista, California, where his father now resided. The subject soon found steady work, married, and fathered a son, but within a couple of years, had fallen back on his old ways.

Coupla hours later, batter up, home run. 'Cept I ain't ready to go no more, and it ain't just the thoughta that Hill waitin' for me neither. Last thing I seen was that boy's father glarin' at me, hatin' me for what I done to his boy, wishin' me dead ten times over.

"I'm sorry."

The police came later that night. I wondered how they had found us. They left us lying there for a really long time while they walked around doing their work. They talked about how tragic it was. Tragic. That was the word they kept using. I kept hoping with all my might that it was just a nightmare. I tried and tried and tried to wake up, but I couldn't. I just lay there, memories spilling out of my head, like the blood I'd felt trickling down my neck. My little brother's birth. Holidays. Birthdays. School. Learning how to ride a bike. Learning how to drive. My friends. The girl I wanted to ask out. I thought about the future that would never be. I would never have a job, go to college, get married, have children or grandchildren. It felt like forever before they put us in those bags and loaded our bodies into the van.

It is believed that the subject's intense anger and hostility toward living things was engendered by the endless cycle of trauma and abuse, which began while he was still in his mother's womb. The subject exhibited violent tendencies at an uncommonly young age. As an adolescent, he took immense pleasure in torturing and killing neighborhood cats, which led to his first arrest. It was not long before the subject had moved on to humans.

Felt my body thrashin' 'round as the poison seeped in, but my mind was sufferin' more. Them stories y'hear 'bout folks' lives flashin' before their eyes when they're dyin', like a picture show? All true, 'cept there weren't no happy scenes in my picture. Thought 'bout Pa takin' the easy way out by pressin' that shotgun 'gainst his heart and pullin' the trigger. Weren't no easy way for me. Hung on for seventeen minutes. They said sixteen, but that last was the killer, felt like a thousand. Before I know it, they got me stuffed in that giant Ziploc. And I'm gone from this life, for good, just like that, headed for that Hill.

In 1975, the subject was incarcerated for the voluntary manslaughter of his oldest brother's roommate. The victim was pummeled to death, allegedly without provocation, while the subject mocked him for being unmanly. The subject then cut off the victim's hair, before dousing him with lighter fluid and throwing matches on him. At the scene, the subject claimed he was acting in self-defense on behalf of the victim's wife, alleging that the victim had threatened her with a knife. The subject later retracted his statement, shifting the blame onto his brother, claiming he had only confessed to protect him. It was a maneuver that would be repeated, with a different brother, three years down the road. Despite repeated warnings that the subject was mentally unstable, he was paroled in January of 1978. Five months and twenty-six days later, he would kill again.

But I wasn't dead. Not inside.

MYIAGROS

It enters the room at 10:15 on the dot every morning, flitting about for several minutes before hovering over my perishing body. I wait for it to alight and pounce on what remains of my sanity.

It touches down on my chin, before springing to the entrance of my right ear canal, where it continues to hover for several more minutes. There was a time when I would attempt to shoo it away, but it proved to be futile. I remain motionless, as it surveys the area, plotting its incursion. The maddening ritual has been going on for so long I have lost track of the days, but I am certain that the creature has surpassed the average lifespan of its species.

I never regretted being single and childless, until the illness came and I realized I would be facing it alone. My three older siblings, none of whom had bred, began dying off five years ago. My parents, who were not paragons of support to begin with, had been gone for ages. I had no other living relatives, and my surviving friends were all indisposed, insane, or dead. Not to mention estranged, as a result of my maladjustment. Ever the deluded know-it-all, I had convinced myself that I was a free and conscience being, when in truth, my entire life was a series of myopic and confining decisions.

The life I had chosen was precarious at best. I was always in the moment, never looking back or forward, my abstracted eyes perpetually locked on the pavement markings rather than the road ahead. I was not born to be chained to a routine occupation, drifting through the days with no expectations, although I was strangely envious of people who were. It had to be easier experiencing life on autopilot, like the mentally challenged, who knew of no other existence than what fate had handed them. Painting had infected me in adolescence, and although I had undeniable talent, I lacked self-confidence and ambition. In hindsight, I can clearly see that I was more enamored by the idea of being an artist than actually being one. I was terrified of the responsibility and potential criticism that would come with success. It was much safer and less painful to lackadaisically flirt with the dream than to capture it. I was prolific to a fault, but remiss in marketing myself, allowing a false sense of humility and the fear of rejection to dictate my course, which would ultimately lead to an impasse. I was like a boxer who would apologize for his fighting skills before stepping into the ring. When opportunities did come along, I would subconsciously sabotage them, finding some lame excuse or another to remain ensconced in obscurity. In my youth, I thought time was limitless, and that fame – on my ill-defined terms – would eventually materialize. All I had to do was paint, and cling to my contradictory and paralyzing ideals. Then five years went by, then five more, and so on. Now here I am — broke, broken, alone, no achievements to speak of, trapped in an infinite moribund state, and physically incapable of taking my own life, which would be the most logical and merciful course of action.

The creature is now resting on my left nasolabial fold, rubbing its disease-ridden legs together so it can better taste the residue from my breakfast. I glance down at it. It stops cleaning itself, shifts its body clockwise, and scurries up my cheek toward my nose, dropping feces along the way. Its compound eyes meet and lock with mine, but *I see it* better than it sees me. Thrown by my composure, it takes flight and zooms around the room before returning to my right ear. It repeats the cycle over and over again, while I remain frozen the entire time. It is a battle of wills I refuse to lose. I have long resigned myself to the fact that Death will come when It is ready, and I cannot persuade It to come sooner. In the intervening time, I wait and wither, in deafening silence, as air gushes through the creature's spiracles, releasing what would be a merciless buzzing sound to the average ear. My zygomatic muscles flex, resulting in a smug grin. I am grateful, at least, that the illness has annihilated my hearing. I take comfort in knowing that when I do expire, the creature will be completely powerless and *I* will be victorious.

When I reached the midpoint of my shortsighted journey, I found life-sustaining gratification in isolation and alienating whomever I could. Not having to answer to anyone but the Muse, I would while away the hours painting up a storm. Incorrigible and insufferable, even to myself, some of my best work was done during that self-imposed purdah. Of course, no one but the cat ever saw that work. While my estranged friends and family would invariably forgive my unforgivable behavior, I would invariably serve up five more reasons for

27

them to keep their distance. It was not long before they gave up and vanished altogether. I thought I was overjoyed to be rid of them. I was not. I am not.

I always knew I would be alone and destitute in my later years, but never imagined I would be ravaged by such an insidious and merciless disease. As is my wont, I had painted myself into a corner. Only now, that corner was a precipice with an abysmal drop. I had no choice but to volunteer for the institute's program, putting myself at the mercy of these mad scientists. I take that back, I did have a choice. I could have killed myself immediately after the diagnosis and not suffered one moment of the living hell that has become my existence. All I had to do was ingest the pharmacopeia in my medicine cabinet, or hang myself with a belt, or both. Instead, I allowed my notorious lack of ambition and fears of failure and commitment to call the shots, my incurable emotional disabilities handing down an infinite sentence of incurable physical disability. After all, death is the ultimate commitment, is it not?

I feel an implosion within my head, as though it has been lanced. A warm, tingly fluid gushes through my cranium, as pitch blackness devours the room. I cannot see, or move from the neck down, but I can hear. For the first time in ages, *I can hear*. I am surely dreaming, must have lost consciousness. I close my eyes and hear a crescendo buzzing sound, indicating that the creature is closing in again. I feel three pairs of legs scaling the bridge of my nose. I instinctively open my eyes, only to be met by glaring darkness. I attempt to swat at the creature, but remain paralyzed. Slamming my eyelids shut, I am viciously assaulted by a blinding light, while simultaneously realizing that my ability to move has been restored. I must be trapped in a lucid nightmare. There is no other explanation. The buzzing sound has now reached deafening decibel levels. The pain in my tympanic membranes is *unbearable*. I place my hands over my ears and scream.

I should have married Dana. She was my soulmate, as she used to say. I understand that now, but at the time, the term soulmate was an insult to my self-proclaimed genius. What an arrogant fool I was. Where most people would have found contentment and security, I saw confinement and danger. I was distrustful of her forbearance and unconditional love, the latter of which felt oppressive, with no blame whatsoever on her part. She could not have been more agreeable and less demanding. She wanted to settle in, not down. I wanted that as well, only a decade too late. By the time I came around, her heart belonged to another, who would mistreat it worse than I had, if that were possible. She wanted a child – one, not five. I could have given her that. Especially after all she had tolerated and done in my behalf. She and that child, now well into adulthood, would be seeing to my deteriorating health. I would not be on a rotting limb, my lot dictated by a ring of nameless, faceless, soulless quacks to whom I am a laboratory animal of the lowest form. I would be surrounded by compassion and love, rather than negligence and apathy. I would go so far as to say that if I wanted to bring an end to my suffering, Dana would not only understand, but help make it happen as well. I have never known a more selfless, humane, and loyal person. When I learned about her suicide five years ago, I was rendered permanently inconsolable and tormented by the likelihood that fate would have been kinder to us both if I had made her my wife. Perhaps it is merely a desperate delusion born from guilt and regret, but I believe I could have become the man she deserved. Over the years I had heard stories about her brief but miserable marriage and ensuing failed relationships. She never did have that child she wanted. She would have made a wonderful parent.

I awaken on what I assume to be the following day, but it is later than my usual rising time. By now, I would have showered and eaten breakfast, but I am neither washed nor fed. What a peculiar nightmare that was, its grotesque realism still fresh in my mind. There is only one certainty in a world that has become certainly uncertain. I prepare myself for the creature's entrance and the daily ceremonial dance. I must admit that, although it is maddening, I have grown accustomed and would feel incomplete without it. I hear it coming. Wait, I *hear* it coming? How is that possible? I must still be asleep. Disoriented and panicking, I grab the letter opener from the nightstand and jab it into my right thigh, wincing in unmistakably *real* pain. The startling disorientation combined with the crushing buzzing sound is *sheer torture*.

The game has changed, but how and why? I do not know if I am dead or alive, but it is clear that I have entered another state of purgatory, one in which the creature is holding the cards. The question is, how long will I remain here?

A SCAR IS BORNE

Norman first encountered Esther via a cleverly written Facebook message, directing him to her SoundCloud page, where he found an assortment of songs, mostly average, with one real earsore that was so atrocious he howled with laughter despite himself. Maintaining a personal profile on the social networking site meant receiving thousands of emails a week from wannabe rockstars, imploring the legendary Norman Marko to sign them to his label and make them rich and famous, regardless of their talent or lack thereof. Norman was thankful for the opportunities he had been given early on in his career, and vowed to pay it forward, which was why he would take the time to read every message that landed in his inbox. Although he did see a measure of potential in Esther, if it weren't for the suggestive photographs and her moxie, he wouldn't have made it through the first track. She was an attractive woman. Not unusually so, but compared to his longtime former supermodel girlfriend, who was transmogrifying into his late mother? There was a subtle disquieting look in Esther's eyes that screamed, *"Run as far away as you can, as fast as you can, you stupid fuck! I will destroy your life, and you will never be able to get rid of me!"* Despite what Norman's gut was telling him, his dick and ego always called the shots. He was going to be 50 next month, a thought that made him want to fellate a shotgun to completion. Maybe a roll in the hay with a woman half his age would boost his perishing self-esteem, which his shrewish girlfriend had been abrading for the past decade. Without giving it another thought, he dialed the phone number included in the email. Since it was a Saturday night, he wasn't sure if Esther would answer. When she did, after a single ring, he hadn't a single doubt about calling. Speaking with her was merely an extension of her email communication, a rarity in the often deceptive Petri dish of social media. After chatting about his record label and her music, they agreed to meet for lunch that Wednesday, at the restaurant at Chateau Marmont, where Norman kept a suite.

When Norman arrived at the restaurant, ten minutes late, Esther was sitting at a table near the front. She was more beautiful in person than in her photos and had the most striking green eyes. As she stood up, he noticed she wasn't wearing any undergarments beneath her skintight dress. Norman felt his cock pulsate. She extended her hand, and through a disarming smile, thanked him for agreeing to meet her. He was instantly and inexplicably captivated. Even though they hadn't exchanged more than 30 minutes of dialogue, he knew she was the woman he was destined to be with. He thought himself mad for allowing the notion to seep into his mind, but Esther was clearly the cure for the disease of a life to which he had condemned himself. He thanked a god he didn't believe in for that message she had sent.

An hour later, they were lying on the California king in Norman's suite, moments away from sealing the deal. As usual, he'd had a dessertspoon of cocaine for breakfast and knocked back ten too many highballs at lunch. Coupled with the frigidity his girlfriend had been heaping on him for as long as he could recall, he was unable to resist Esther's intrepid come-ons. She might as well have sucked him off under the table as he picked away at his Caesar Salad. The foreplay was brief, almost a formality, like rushing through grace before digging into a mouthwatering meal. It consisted of a single, albeit passionate French kiss. Then Norman peeled off her painted-on dress and took her perky tits into his mouth, licking and sucking aggressively, while stroking her clitoris with his forefinger. She was even more aroused than she had let on. It was all he could do to refrain from shooting his load, and she hadn't even touched him where it counted yet. After clumsily freeing himself from his leather pants, he flipped her over, pulled her plump ass toward him, and rammed his painfully erect cock into her succulent young pussy. He felt a clamping sensation, as though a set of tiny teeth had grabbed hold of his manhood, and was overwhelmed by an unfathomable feeling of release, which transcended the feeling of release that came with climaxing. Esther let out a triumphant moan, tightened her grip, and ordered Norman to get what he came for. Thrusting, as though his body had been hijacked by a sexual demon, he couldn't fuck her hard enough or fast enough. All sensation went directly to his dick, which felt as if it were going to explode. Yet, at the same time, ejaculation felt impossible. When he finally did cum, 30 minutes later, it was *alchemical*, like no other orgasm he had experienced before. That was not sex, *it was a rebirth*. Norman Marko was a changed man. He decided right then and there that he was going to leave his girlfriend for Esther and make her a star. He knew it was wrong in every possible way, and that he would take loads of flak from his friends, but he didn't care. He felt *alive* for the first time in years.

Esther walked away from the experience equally euphoric, but for different reasons. She had found the next rung on her ladder to stardom, and it was the most promising rung yet. Norman not only owned a critically acclaimed independent record label, but was also the founder, guitarist, and songwriter of Prisoner's Cinema, an immortal band that had ruled the music industry globally for the duration of the 80s and well into the 90s. It didn't matter that they hadn't recorded any new material in over a decade. Their place in the rock pantheon was eternally sealed. Of course, like the numerous other rungs that had come before, if a better opportunity presented itself, Esther would drop Norman as quickly as she had jumped in the sack with him. She wasn't an inherently evil person, but the years she had spent in the trenches, struggling and yearning to reach the top, had definitely hardened her. She was more determined than ever to succeed. At 30, she was nearing the popstar expiration date, and would only be able to pass for 25 for so long. Sure, Norman was a notorious drunk and philanderer who was old enough to be her father, but he was also world-famous, filthy rich, and well-connected. He could not only launch her career, but provide financial support as well. She was done and then some waiting on those disrespectful morons in that shithole of a nightclub, busting her back to make ends meet and still coming up short. She had already milked Grandma dry and wouldn't give Dad the satisfaction of asking for his help. He would only tell her to "Give up on that crazy dream of yours and come home!" No goddamn way. Going back to North Dakota was certain death. She was staying put, and Norman Marko would be her all-inclusive ticket. She was going to sink her claws and fangs deep into his soul, and hang on for as long as necessary.

One week after that seemingly predestined yet purely calculated rendezvous, at the new rung's insistence, Esther walked out on her dead-end job and vacated her rundown apartment in East Hollywood. Then she moved herself and meager possessions into Norman's posh suite at the Chateau Marmont. It had been a place of refuge during the later and more volatile years of his previous relationship. Now, he was going to make a home of it with the angel who had resuscitated him from emotional death. He had returned to the sentient state of his youth and found himself *wanting* to feel, for a change. He no longer needed the escape hatch chemicals had provided for most of his adult life. He had Esther, who was better than any mood-enhancing or numbing drug. She complemented him superbly, and the sex was not only preternatural, but salubrious, with each orgasm making him more mentally robust. It was as if her vagina were injecting him with a potent psychical analeptic.

For Esther, she was finally living as she was meant to all along, and would *never* return to the underclass again. She called home to report, in a gleefully smug tone, that she had been signed to a label and would be recording her first official album. She also told them that "the people at the label" had rented her a swank new apartment, neglecting to mention that it was being shared, along with her bed, with her new sugar daddy, who was only three years younger than her father. Her family was overjoyed, especially Grandma, who had donated every penny of her savings to Esther and the pursuit of her dream. Although Dad and Auntie had serious doubts that Esther would ever achieve fame, Grandma never stopped believing.

Norman had no family, but did gush about Esther to his friends, who were understandably suspicious. His best friend, in particular, pulled no punches when expressing his distrust. Had Norman completely lost his mind? He needed to get a grip and fast! What the hell was he thinking, moving some strange chick into his place one week after he had met her? What did he really know about her, aside from what he had read on her social media profiles, which was probably all bullshit anyway? She was obviously an opportunist of the worst kind, and the fact that she had fucked him just one hour after meeting him meant she was a slut too. Who knows how many other guys she had spread her legs for? A chick like that could never be trusted. Norman wrote it all off as jealousy, but knew deep down that his friend's concerns were not unfounded.

The next two months were spent planning assiduously for Esther's debut, which would be a seven-track EP consisting of dramatically reworked versions of what Norman considered to be her best material. Part of that planning involved calling in favors. Norman had always been likeable and generous with others, and was worshipped by the latest generation of rockstars. It only took one call to secure a renowned producer, and three more calls to secure three equally renowned musicians to serve as Esther's backup band. Although Esther's lyrics were rather juvenile and self-pitying, the martyr shtick was all the rage with teenage girls and younger women, who accounted for a significant portion of her potential fans. With hopes of making the album more appealing to audiences beyond that demographic, Norman fine-tuned and rearranged the music, so it would not only complement, but enhance the lyrics. No one could resist a catchy hook, and he made sure there were plenty. Esther's voice might be an acquired taste, but it was certainly unique, and she was just as talented as the female singers who were dominating the charts and airwaves — which wasn't saying much, he hated to admit. No matter, though. With the dream team he had enlisted and the available technology, the EP was destined to be a smash hit. Norman had no doubt.

The recording process was a welcome departure from the self-destructive hamster wheel Norman had been lumbering on. It felt incredible to be back in the studio, creating music with other humans, rather than conducting mind-numbing business behind a computer or phone screen. Esther's drive, professionalism, and amenability were admirable, more than compensating for her questionable talent. She was ecstatic, and kept expressing her heartfelt gratitude to Norman, which made him feel like a giant. Through her, he was being given another chance to shine.

Three months later, the EP, entitled *Hecate*, was ready to unleash. During the mixing and mastering process, Norman had hired a team of experts to craft Esther's image: a plastic surgeon who lifted her brow, tapered the nose, augmented her modest bosom, and sucked out her saddlebags, a stylist who gave her a lush mane of auburn hair extensions, aquamarine contact lenses, metamorphic facial makeup, and elaborate handmade costumes, and an ace publicist who changed her name to Vida LeBeau, contrived a hard-luck story about her upbringing in rural North Dakota, trimmed five years from her age, and began generating buzz about the new queen who was going to knock Lady Gaga off her throne. Along with the names attached to the album, and the magic everyone had worked in the studio and beyond, Esther was a shoo-in to be the music industry's next It Girl. She looked and sounded like the superstar she was, and the world would surely bow before her as soon as they heard the opening track.

Unfortunately, that wasn't how it played out. Far from it. The press and public didn't hear what Norman was hearing, because they weren't reverentially in love with Esther. Their hearing wasn't clouded by intense personal feelings, as Norman's was. It was a matter of fact that Esther was marginally talented, at best, and painfully self-conscious. All the trickery in the world couldn't hide it. The band sounded magnificent, but Esther's voice was undeniably annoying, worsened by her embarrassingly affected lyrics. Then there were those critics who saw the album for what it truly was, and didn't mince words. Davis Funk, a journalist who had championed Norman's creative efforts throughout his career, summarized it spitefully, albeit honestly:

THE LEGENDARY NORMAN MARKO OF THE ALMIGHTY PRISONER'S CINEMA FALLS FLAT IN HIS ATTEMPT TO FORCE HIS TALENTLESS CONCUBINE ON THE MASSES

A total of 553 CDs were sold, mostly to diehard fans of Norman. They claimed to absolutely love the album, but he knew damn well they were merely kissing his ass. Besides a negligible following garnered via social media, Esther was still trapped in obscurity.

When her debut failed to make a splash and was torn apart by the critics, Esther's chronic mental and emotional issues reared their head for the first time. It marked a bleak turning point for the blissful couple, with Norman becoming Esther's whipping boy. He had promised to make her a superstar, and when that didn't happen, she viewed it as an unforgivable act of betrayal, taking every opportunity to remind him. Her Psychology 101 defense mechanism quickly became pathological and borderline abusive. Whenever life didn't go as Esther wanted, it was all Norman's fault, even though he was rarely to blame. Although there were veiled indications at the beginning, Norman had no idea that his truelove suffered from a plethora of severe psychological problems, including textbook cases of Narcissistic and Histrionic Personality Disorders. Once again, his gut told him to split before it was too late, but he was crazy about her, and his overpowering conscience would never allow him to abandon her. Instead, he rationalized her behavior. He had indeed broken his promise, which gave her every right to be angry at him. Having one's music unappreciated and worse yet, panned could be devastating. Although he had never been subjected to it himself, he was deeply sympathetic. Esther's dream had been crushed, before it had the slightest chance to hatch. It was no wonder she was descending into an abysmal depression. It was his duty to stick by her side and do whatever he could to help.

Despite Norman's unflagging devotion, Esther's condition only worsened. Even the most competent doctors and strongest medications couldn't alleviate her despair. Before long, the megrims began to rub off on Norman. He put up a valiant fight, but soon found himself falling back into that self-loathing void he had been trapped in prior to meeting Esther. The survivor in him wanted to run like hell, but the empath in him feared she would seriously harm or kill herself if he did. He figured her for an attempter rather than a doer, but what if he was mistaken?

One evening, three months into the slough of despond, Esther came into Norman's office and announced that she was ready to make another record. She had been composing lyrics furiously throughout her nervous breakdown, resulting in a 10-song concept album, with the concept being "Injustice." Claiming to know what went wrong with the EP, she demanded to have more control and insisted on taking her sound in a different direction, more pop than rock. More commercial and accessible, that is. She also insisted that in the public eye she and Norman act as though their relationship was strictly professional, without a trace of romance. She was going to make it on her own merits, goddamn it, and would *never* be written off as *anyone's* concubine *ever again*. Staring into her entrancing eyes, Norman could see that the darkness had lifted, almost as if it had never landed. He despised pop music and all that it stood for, but enthusiastically bowed to her demands, knowing he would ultimately be in control anyway. Not to mention footing the bill to make and promote the album, as well as writing most of the music. There went *making it on her own merits*. He would have agreed to *anything* to pull her back into the light, though. Yes, she could be insufferable, but he loved her madly and hated to see her withering away. Plus, it was a second chance to deliver on that promise he had made. Vida LeBeau was going to be a star.

After polishing the lyrics, Norman helped Esther compose the music, allowing her to believe that she was doing most of the work. As soon as the last note was written, they returned to the studio, with a brand new producer and backup band. Esther had fired and denounced the first batch, claiming they were to blame for the EP's failure, destroying Norman's relationships with them in the process. She insisted that a complete departure from the catastrophic debut was the only way to proceed and more important, *succeed*. Although Norman wasn't pleased with her behavior or where the project was going artistically, he indulged Esther's every whim, while doing his best to salvage the ever putrefying stinker along the way. He was so grateful to see the spark returning to her eyes he was willing to make sacrifices. Even if that meant putting up with her drama, eating platefuls of invective shit, betraying his beliefs, and losing longtime friends.

Five months later, the album was released, and met with mixed reviews, but phenomenal sales. It also swept up every trophy that mattered when the awards shows rolled around. A sold-out, multi-city North American tour followed, with plans underway for the rest of the world. Esther was a superstar. Norman was not only thrilled, but immensely relieved. With Esther's dream now realized, she would finally be happy, and their relationship would only improve.

Or so he thought. Ever the self-pitying diva, Esther chose to wallow in the negative, instead of basking in the glory and appreciating the golden horseshoe that had been wedged up her ass. She became increasingly paranoid and was plagued with persecutory delusions. The media were spreading lies about her, other artists were copying her, and no matter how much praise she *did* receive – from both the press and fans – it was never enough to override the criticism, with which she was obsessed. Fearing the backlash if he dared to question any of it, Norman remained a pillar of support, which only worsened her malady. Esther had metamorphosed into a monster, and Norman was partially responsible through his enablement. Rather than face the hideous truth and his role in its creation, he returned to booze, drugs, and infidelity. He drank, smoked, snorted, and fucked his way through the wretched days, believing it was the only way to deal with the fix he had gotten himself into. Who knew he could wind up in a train wreck more fatal than the previous?

To pour acid onto the festering wound, Norman eloped with Esther on the weekend of her 32nd – or rather, third 25th – birthday. He was already doomed anyway. At least by making it legal, he could recoup some of the fortune he had sunken into her and ease his way back into the spotlight via her coattails. He did write every note of the music, after all, even though it was credited to her. His thumbprint was all over that multiplatinum seller, a fact that seemed to be lost on everyone who had heard it. It was what made Norman invaluable to Esther, especially now that there were expectations. If her career was ever going to progress beyond that album, she needed him more than ever. More important, she needed him to believe it was the other way around, which was why she alienated him from his loved ones, which in his case were his friends. Employing the classic abusive relationship maneuver, she convinced her broken husband that she was the only person in his life who truly cared about him. The fragile, chemical-induced state he had fallen back into made him more manipulable than ever. Drowning in his vices and her witchcraft, he was blind to her wiles and mind games, which were slowly annihilating him. The daily excoriations were damaging enough on their own. When combined with the nightly seductions, it was a recipe for a noxious headfuck. The only "saving grace" was that she no longer cared if the public knew about their relationship. She was now infinitely more famous than her husband and almost as wealthy. No journalist would have the balls to question her musical prowess or label her a kept woman, *ever again*. She not only wore the pants, but the crown as well.

Being disgustingly rich and worshipped worldwide wasn't enough for Esther. She also had a sadistic need to smash her success in the faces of others, especially those goddamn dream-killers who had doubted her. When leaving the family farm in North Dakota, she had sworn wrathfully to her father, aunt, cousins, and other naysayers that she would be living in a Beverly Hills mansion by the end of the decade. It was the only missing piece in her popstar dream puzzle. Norman would have preferred residing in a third world nation over that pretentious bubble, but to please his bride, he acquiesced and purchased a colossal estate with a 23,000 square-foot house. Esther referred to it as their "happy home." For Norman, it felt more like a stygian dungeon, which was why he kept his suite at the hotel, a decision that resulted in an unprecedentedly nasty altercation with Esther. While he did plan on bringing plenty of women there to fuck, that wasn't his primary motive for holding on to the place. As he explained to Esther, he needed a familiar and sequestered working environment conducive to creativity. Now more than ever, since he was responsible for *her* career, as well as his own. Esther was furious it hadn't been her call, but was forced to yield, albeit grudgingly.

Three more hit albums came over the next two years, each more favorably received than the previous, with journalists praising the level of maturity and depth in the lyrics. No, Esther hadn't miraculously developed songwriting skills. Norman was now writing the lyrics in addition to the music. Esther was so caught up in being famous she had no time for the creation process anymore. Even getting her into the studio to record vocals was an ordeal. She preferred acting in films, making appearances on talk shows, and doing product endorsements. The remainder of her alleged work time was pissed away on Facebook, Twitter, and Instagram, whining about her so-called "cursed life" and posting cadaverously retouched selfies showing her living the highlife. As usual, Norman picked up the slack. At an age when most musicians would be categorized as past their prime, his otherworldly talents only continued to flourish. He had always said that misery and conflict were the keys to writing great songs, and he certainly had no shortage of either being married to Esther. Plus, he was having a blast being a closet female popstar, although he never would have admitted that to any creature capable of comprehending human language.

As for their marriage, it had been reduced to the strictly professional status they had once feigned in the public eye. It was a business arrangement, pure and simple, with Esther getting the better end of the deal. Norman was spending his days holed up in his suite, deteriorating personally yet thriving artistically, while Esther was busy partying, squandering his money, and being idolized. Both were sleeping with other people, and hadn't shared a bed with each other in months. Despite it all, Norman continued to feel intense love for his wife, as well as a sense of obligation. He wanted her to remain successful, and became indignant when the press badmouthed her, going so far as to threaten their lives if they didn't recant their disparaging words. His long estranged friends, who were easing their way back into his life, were gravely concerned and begged him to leave Esther before he completely disintegrated. Even though he knew the misalliance was irreparably fractured, walking away was an idea his drug-soaked mind couldn't begin to comprehend, let alone consider. Esther needed him and always would. He could never turn his back on her. It was a terminal situation that seemed destined to carry on indefinitely, unless an act of supernature intervened.

In September, Vida LeBeau's live album, *Vida! Live In Tangier,* was released. To promote the sham, which featured overdubbed vocals recorded in a Los Angeles studio, Esther went to New York for a week to hit the late night and talk show circuit. Norman was supposed to accompany her, for the sake of appearances, but could never tolerate her divacity in those settings and conveniently "fell ill" the day they were scheduled to depart. In her absence, he stayed at the Beverly Hills mansion, drugging and fucking himself into oblivion. On the day Esther was due to return, he was reading the news on his computer, nursing his fifth Irish coffee, when the following headline nearly knocked him out of his swivel chair:

THE SHOCKING TRUTH ABOUT VIDA LEBEAU EXPOSED!

After reading every mortifying word of the article, he began to retch violently. Interspersed among a heap of libelous dirt were irrefutable facts: Esther's real name and age, the truth about her upbringing, the real story behind her stellar career and wildly popular music... *all of it*. For a split second, Norman wondered how on earth they could have found out, but then admitted to himself that the only real shocker was that it hadn't happened sooner. Esther had a multitude of enemies, between Norman's friends and the myriad people she had fucked over on her warpath to stardom. Any of them had every reason and right to blab to the press. Vida LeBeau was through, a victim of her own ego and mendacity. While Norman was glad he didn't have to be the bearer of the unthinkable news, the protector in him was desperate to console Esther.

Meanwhile, on an airplane flying miles above the Midwest, Esther was on the verge of losing it. Since boarding the flight, people had been staring at her and whispering, and not in the usual star-struck manner. After hearing the woman behind her remark, "I always knew she was older than she claimed to be," Esther powered up her tablet and went online using the wifi provided for the first-class passengers. The instant the homepage loaded, she was knocked sideways by the same haymaker of a headline Norman had seen. She hadn't even finished the first humiliating paragraph before snapping into a full-scale tantrum, writhing in her seat and screaming obscenity-laden threats at the top of her lungs. Believing it was a possible terrorist attack, all five flight attendants rushed to the front of the plane, where they were met with an onslaught of misplaced vitriol. Realizing it was merely a histrionic performance by a disgraced prima donna, they ordered Esther to calm down, or else they would be forced to physically restrain her. She responded by telling them to, "Go ahead and try, you plebian cunts! I dare you!" Followed by the proverbial, "Do you know who I am?" Rounded off with, "I'll have you all fired and charged with assault!" Then she demanded a vodka tonic to wash down her Xanax.

As the pill and booze began to work their magic, Esther analyzed her predicament, which was entirely self-induced, although she never would have admitted that. She couldn't decide what was worse: the untruths they were propagating or the unearthing of the truths she had been struggling to hide. Not only from others, but herself as well. It had always been easy to fool the gullible fans and most of the press, but she could *never* fool herself, and *that* was the source of her unrelenting anguish. Her unmarketable reality had been lurking all along, threatening to invalidate her. Now, it was being smashed into her face, like a night soil pie. She was not the strong, original, independent artist she vehemently claimed to be. She was a feeble, dangerously neurotic, and marginally talented fabrication who was entirely reliant upon Norman. Without him, there would be no career or any of the perks that came with it. There was no denying it: beneath the elaborate veneer, Esther was a charlatan and glorified prostitute, just like her mother. *"How dare they?"* she screamed at the peanut gallery in her swollen head. *"Someone is going to pay for what those ungrateful, traitorous maggots have done!"* That someone would be Norman. Even though he was only guilty of enabling her, she blamed him entirely, for everything, always. Displacement came as naturally to Esther as breathing, and could reach masturbatory levels when she was off her meds. After knocking back three more drinks, she dozed off for the remainder of the flight, dreaming about how she would exact her revenge.

The instant the plane landed, Esther steamrolled her way to the door, shoving aside an elderly woman in a wheelchair. As she plowed through the crowded terminal, her chauffeur was nowhere in sight, and she hadn't the patience to wait for him, especially with everyone staring at her. After retrieving her luggage from the carousel, she pounced on the first cab she spotted – shoving aside a crying toddler clinging to his mommy's hand – and ordered the driver to step on it. She couldn't wait to get home and crush Norman with her vindictive rage.

Norman had been trying to reach Esther for two hours, with every call going straight to her voicemail. She wasn't responding to his texts either. He was now sick with worry, and feared she might have harmed herself. He was just about to head to the airport when he heard a car door slam shut outside. Rushing to the master bedroom window to investigate, he heard the front door slam shut. She was home and safe. He ran downstairs to greet her and was met with a backhand to the face, followed by a sharp slap to the other side as he lost his footing from the initial blow. It was the first time she had ever laid a hand on him. No matter how ugly it had gotten over the years, she had never resorted to physical abuse. Before he could say a word, she tore into him with a barrage of revilement designed to rip out his heart and castrate him, with *"I wish you were dead!"* as the coup de grace.

Instead of instinctively firing back, physically or verbally, Norman glowered at the poisonous, piteous creature standing in front of him and realized he was finally free. Overcome by that same feeling of release he had experienced during their first sexual encounter, the spell had been lifted and Esther was powerless. He smiled victoriously at the mortal he had mistaken for his savior, then grabbed and carried her out the back door, as she clawed, flailed, and screamed idle threats. When he reached the pool, he walked down the steps and plunged his bane into the tepid water. Wrapping his hands firmly around her throat, he held her under, as bubbles of fury, salvation, and the desperate need to survive surrounded them. Those entrancing green eyes struggled to subjugate him once more, as she took her final breath. Leaving her lifeless body floating toward the hot tub, he walked back into the house and emerged moments later, carrying a 50-pound Weider plate with a chain attached. Calmly positioning himself at the edge of the rock structure near the deep end, he secured the anchor around his waist and fell headfirst toward the wraith staring up at him.

NARCOLEPTIC SHRINK

The moment I met Bradley, I knew the job would be unprecedentedly challenging. I'd dealt with my share of difficult bosses, but he and I couldn't have been less temperamentally compatible. While I considered myself more *truly* tolerant than the average person, I knew from experience that certain people were better off avoiding each other, rather than even attempting to get along. I'd been hired, sight unseen, thanks to a glowing recommendation from my friend Tom. I felt a gnawing sense of foreboding, but after being unemployed for a year, I was beyond relieved to be working again.

My first task, on my first day, was to move a third desk into the already cramped junior managers' office. A breeze compared to my second task, which was to listen to *Narcoleptic Shrink*, the most recent album from Bradley's top client, an Eastern European Polka Metal band called Futile Onanist & The Flaccid Putz. As the torturously monotonous racket assaulted my tympanic membranes, I was certain *I would need a shrink* to cope with the trauma caused by the experience. To each his own, but I found it hard to believe that any creature with the ability to hear could find the music remotely appealing. When the final song came to its merciful end, I couldn't yank out the earbuds quickly enough. I looked up and saw Bradley standing in the doorway with a cocky grin on his face.

"What do you think?" he asked in a presumptuous tone, as though he already knew my answer and that it would be favorable.

If I'm honest, I wondered, *will I be given the axe? Maybe my honesty will be rewarded? Or maybe it's a test? It has to be.*

"I think it may be the worst music… and I use that term loosely… I've ever heard in my life," I replied, matter-of-factly.

Finn, one of the junior managers at the firm, burst into laughter on the other side of the room, abruptly stopping when Bradley glared at him.

"Well," Bradley said condescendingly, with a wry face and fake laugh, "that's why *I'm* the manager and *you're* just the junior manager in training. Don't worry, there's hope for you yet. I just need to teach your ear to know genius when you hear it."

He was clearly one of those people who equated his position with supreme knowledge. I'd encountered many while working various jobs in the entertainment industry. They were as purblind as the gullible fans that automatically correlated stardom with rare and phenomenal talent. You know the type: *"S/he has to be the best or s/he wouldn't be a star!"* which anyone with half a brain knows is bullshit. My gut instinct was to fire back at Bradley with: "My ear is just fine, fuck you very much, and if that's *your* idea of genius, maybe *I* should be training *you*." But, as I mentioned, I needed the job.

"Whatever you say," I replied, forcing myself to smile. "You're the boss."

"That's right," he scoffed. Then he pointed toward a tower of boxes sitting in the corner near Finn's desk. "See those boxes over there? It's stuff that wouldn't fit in *my Beverly Hills mansion* anymore. Move them to the storage closet before lunch. Don't drop any of them either. There are breakables worth a fortune."

"Will do," I said cheerfully, when I really felt like saying, *"Are you fucking kidding, you passive-aggressive cunt?"* The boxes were packed beyond capacity and obviously punishingly heavy, not to mention stacked from floor to ceiling. Then there was the way he threw the words "my Beverly Hills mansion" into my face, as if to remind me that I was merely some broke peon.

"When you're done with that," he said, scratching at a piece of cellulose tape on the door's strike plate, "do whatever's necessary to remove this piece of tape. It doesn't belong here and I'm tired of looking at it." Then he retreated to his own office, which was three times the size of the junior managers'.

"That was effin brilliant!" Finn giggled, tossing a Snickers bar across the room. "Mad props for putting that twerp and his crappy client in their place!"

"I was only being honest," I said, catching the treat and tearing open the wrapper. "For a moment there, I thought it was a test. Or maybe a joke. Those guys are not only devoid of talent, but also insufferably grating. They're his top client?"

"Yep. Pathetic, huh? But they bring in more dough than all his other clients combined. That's the kind of junk that sells nowadays. The music industry's become a total farce."

"Yikes. That's insane. It makes me wonder if I'm cut out to work in the music industry," I said, taking a bite and chewing. "You can swear all you want, by the way. No need for effins, crappy, junk, etc."

"I've been here for two years, and not a day's gone by when I haven't wondered the same about myself," a pleasant voice interjected. It was Julian, the other junior manager, returning from a round of menial errands Bradley had no right to assign. "I always envisioned myself representing acts with a tremendous amount of talent and respectability," he chuckled. "Who knew I would wind up settling for the likes of Futile Onanist & The Flaccid Putz?"

"Dude, you just missed a truly poetic moment!" Finn said, tossing a Snickers bar to Julian.

"I was standing right outside the door and heard the whole exchange," Julian said, catching the candy. "Good on you for speaking your mind, although you do realize that Bradley is going to hold it against you for the rest of your life? Still, good on you."

He was right. That incident set the precedent for my entire stint under Bradley's micromanaging iron fist. A sadistic taskmaster who derived pleasure from crucifying his employees, it was his mission to make every moment in that office as unpleasant as possible. Certifiably paranoid and pathologically controlling, he scrutinized our every move, going so far as to equip our computers with remote access and monitoring software. Along with the most galling idiosyncrasies imaginable, he oozed vampiric poison that sucked the life out of anyone within range. Each morning, when he drove into the underground parking structure, my neck and trapezius muscles would tense up. I couldn't see him arriving, but *knew* he was there, based on my body's reaction. He had the same effect on Julian and Finn, without whom, I never would have lasted ten minutes in that oppressive environment, let alone ten months. They were gems, albeit polar opposites, with introverted Julian providing much needed sanity, and extroverted Finn, much needed levity. How either of them wound up working *under* Bradley was a mystery, since it was obvious they were the brains and balls of the operation. That mystery was solved when I learned Bradley had inherited the business from his deceased father-in-law, a lion of a manager, who had represented some of the most celebrated bands in rock history. As impossible as it seemed, some poor woman had been foolish or desperate enough to marry Bradley. Her name was Belinda, a former model/scenester turned housewife/mother who inexplicably latched onto me. Assuming she was as fucked up as her husband, if not more, I did my best to keep her at arm's length, but to no avail. She would invariably call the office at my lunch hour or right when I was about to leave for the day. Then I'd be forced to listen to the same musty anecdotes about her adolescent escapades with various rockstars and "how awesome the Los Angeles music scene was back in the day." I'd occasionally have lunch with her and her friends, where I'd be dragged into arguments about petty shit that happened before I was even born. She mistakenly believed I was impressed by it all, when in fact, I felt sorry for her. As I got to know her better, I realized she was a decent human being, stagnating in a self-imposed prison. In addition to being married to a shithead like Bradley for half her life, her entire self-worth was based on a romanticized interpretation of a life she had lived decades ago. She was lively and attractive, and beneath the thick rind of baggage and neuroses was untapped potential. I couldn't help wondering what had happened to all the in-between years. While I could appreciate a sprinkling of personal nostalgia every now and then, I viewed yesteryear as an asylum reserved for people whose lives had gone nowhere or to pot in the time since. It seemed wrong that someone like Belinda, who was born with a wealth of gifts and opportunities, would choose to be chained to the past rather than savoring and maximizing the present while looking forward to the future. Maybe it was the only way she could cope with her presumably miserable marriage.

Back to the hellish job itself, I plodded through the exasperating days, which began and ended with an interminable gridlocked commute. Bradley's corrosive nature continued to erode my wellbeing, exacerbated by the fact that I had to remain civil and compliant, no matter what. There is *nothing* more damaging to the spirit than being forced to feign respect for someone you detest, especially when your livelihood depends on it. Tragically, it's the harsh reality for most working stiffs who are stuck in a life-sapping system that never should have been created in the first place. I'd taken the creative path hoping to escape that bleak fate, yet there I was, trapped under the thumb of an ignorant sociopath who should have been running a fast food restaurant, not a firm dedicated to promoting music. Again, needing the job, I had no choice but to endure the unendurable, while reminding myself of the stress and fear that came with being unemployed.

By the Holidays, the unrelenting psychical strain was having an adverse impact on my physical health. In addition to recurring migraines and peptic ulcers, I couldn't remember when I'd last had a restful night's sleep. I wondered if it was worth it. Since dropping out of college five years prior, I'd poured my soul into the entertainment industry, which had always been precarious and sometimes cruel, hoping my diligence would lead to a rewarding career. Maybe I'd be better off seeking employment in a more stable field. I knew that was impossible, though. I had the bug, and as anyone who's ever had it knows, there's no getting rid of it. I decided to suck it up and stick it out through the New Year, then regroup.

On a balmy Monday morning in mid-January, I pulled into the parking structure to find Julian standing in my space, looking uncharacteristically distressed.

"What's up?" I asked, rolling down my window. "Are you okay?"

"Let's go for breakfast," he replied.

"What about Bradley? Isn't he here?"

Julian walked over to the passenger's side and got in. "Not until noon," he said, fastening his seat belt.

"Where to?"

"Jerry's Deli. Finn's already there."

Zipping in and out of the usual cross-town snarl, I asked Julian what was going on, but he refused to talk about it until Finn was present as well.

When we reached the restaurant, 23 minutes later, Finn was sitting in a booth near the back. "So, spill it already, Man!" he said, as Julian and I sat down. "The suspense is killing me!"

The server spotted us and came over with a pot of fresh coffee. "Would you like some coffee?" she asked through a warm smile.

The three of us replied, "Yes, please."

"Are you ready to order?" she asked, filling our cups. "Or do you need more time?"

"More time, please, thanks," Julian replied. Once the server was out of earshot, he cleared his throat and said, "I don't know how to tell you what I'm about to tell you, so I'm just going to say it."

"Yes! Please do!" Finn laughed. "Before I lose my fucking mind here!"

"Bradley has been having an affair with Belinda's 14-year-old niece," Julian blurted out.

"Whaaaaaaat?" Finn said, choking on his coffee.

"Wait, there's more. He's also addicted to teenage pornography. I found a huge stash of photos, videos, and websites on his laptop last night."

"How did you get into his laptop?" I interjected. "I know it's irrelevant, but I'm curious."

"Not as irrelevant as you would think. For some time now, I've suspected he's been embezzling money from the company to support some kind of addiction. Yesterday morning, those suspicions were confirmed when Christy, the assistant manager I know at Chase, called to report questionable activity on our corporate credit accounts, which, if you recall, were opened for emergencies only. Well, over the past several months, Bradley's transferred tons of cash from those accounts to his personal accounts, undoubtedly to fund his porn addiction and god knows what else."

"That sneaky little shit!" Finn said, pounding his fist on the table. "No wonder he's been paying us late every month!"

"As luck would have it," Julian continued, "he left his laptop behind and open when rushing out to catch *Dancing with the Stars* last night. I took the opportunity to search for evidence, and that's when I found the porn and steamy correspondence with Belinda's niece."

"Unreal," I said, attempting to process the news. "I knew he was fucked up, but pedophilia is some serious shit I can't *ever* un-know, now that I know. There's no way I can work for him anymore. He's lucky I'm not taking a baseball bat to his skull."

"I feel the exact same way, believe me," Julian said, emphatically. "Unfortunately, all three of us need to continue working for him and act as though nothing's happened, until I can figure out how to deal with the situation. Embezzlement is bad enough, but pedophilia is a career killer, and our reputations could be on the line as well, because of our association with Bradley."

"You're right, of course," Finn grumbled. "If that arrogant, sick turd walked in here right now, I'd poke out his eyes with my fork."

"I'd chop off his balls with my knife," I added, "and stuff them up his nostrils."

"Furthermore," Julian interjected, "I would like to keep the clients, if possible. Let's face it, Finn, you and I have done most of the work there, anyway. It would be a shame to lose them because of Bradley's fuckup."

"Right again," Finn sighed.

"Have you folks had a chance to decide here?" the waitress asked, approaching the table again.

That morning, Bradley had an appointment with his shrink, absurdly enough, and didn't arrive at the office until 12:35, by which time, Julian, Finn, and I had been there for an hour. He had no clue that his sick secrets had been unearthed. As difficult as each day had been prior to that point, they all paled in comparison to that day and those that followed. I struggled, not only to hold my tongue, but to maintain the mandatory civility and compliance, which now required more effort than ever. The unmitigated lack of respect I had for the man had progressed into homicidal hatred. He must have sensed it too, because my assigned tasks became increasingly tedious and degrading. He also went out of his way to keep me away from the building's other managers, who would offer invaluable advice about working in the industry. Although blind to his own ineptitude, he must have known I would learn far more from them than I could ever learn from him. It was perfectly clear he didn't want me to advance in any way, *in spite of* the promises he had made when I'd been hired. He wanted a galley slave, not a protégé.

After a week, I'd reached my limit. I brought all small talk to a halt, and only spoke to the prick when absolutely necessary. Although I had no intention of quitting, and would continue to do my job as required, I could no longer pretend to like him. My colleagues struggled too, Finn in particular. Like me, he found it impossible to do the dance, and would threaten to walk on a daily basis. Julian talked him out of it every time, assuring him it wouldn't be in his best interest.

Two Sundays after the bolt from the blue, Julian, Finn, and I met up for a late breakfast. Since Bradley strictly prohibited us from taking our lunch breaks together, evenings and weekends were the only opportunities to discuss our entirely non-self-induced plight.

"What's the plan, Dude?" Finn asked Julian. "I've been thinking of creative ways to get canned. At least I could collect unemployment that way."

Julian let out a deep sigh. "I know you guys need your jobs as much as I do, and to protect our careers, the best course of action would be to keep our mouths shut and carry on pretending as though none of this ever happened, but my conscience won't allow that. I think the authorities need to be notified immediately. I'm just trying to figure out if it wouldn't be wiser to place the call anonymously."

"I agree," Finn said, balancing a spoon on his nose, "and the call should definitely be anonymous."

"Will they take the allegations seriously?"

"Probably not," I said, knowing what needed to be done. "I'll make the call *and* say I was the one who discovered the sex crimes. There's no reason to pull you guys into it at all. No one can possibly find you guilty by association if you had no idea what was going on, and being a woman will automatically exonerate me."

"You would do that?" Finn asked in disbelief.

"In a heartbeat."

"Wow! You're one cool chick."

"I can't let you do that," Julian sighed. "It wouldn't be right or fair. I'm the one who dug up this mess and dumped it on you guys, and I should be the one who cleans it up."

"Jesus H. Christ!" Finn snapped, laughing. "Stop being a fucking martyr, already! Seriously, Dude. Her plan makes perfect sense. I don't know about you, but I definitely don't want to be known as *the guy who knew he was working for a pedophile and didn't do jack shit about it*. Ignorance is innocence here. And besides, this is our chance to get that toxic fucker out of our lives for good. Regardless of how it all plays out, how could you *not* want that?"

"Then it's settled?" I asked, smiling.

Julian heaved another deep sigh. "I guess so, but let it be known that I don't feel right about you taking the brunt."

"I'm not taking any brunt. I'm performing a civic duty by turning in a criminal. Someone has to do it, and I'm the best candidate for the job."

"Great!" Finn said. "Now, let's eat! I'm famished!"

The plan was to call the police the following evening, after Bradley had gone home for the day. It would be better to have him picked up at his house instead of the office, where an audience would be present. The other tenants in the building would eventually learn about his perverse crimes, but there was no reason to make an exhibition of the takedown. Not that I cared about humiliating that scumbag, mind you. I simply wanted to make the process as painless as possible for his blameless employees.

When I arrived at work that morning, Bradley and Julian were already there. I could hear them arguing in the junior managers' office.

"I can't believe you deleted the originals *and* the backups!" Julian yelled. "How could you? I spent *hours* working on those documents! *Hours!*"

"Not my problem!" Bradley snapped. "If you had followed orders, I wouldn't have had to delete them! I never told you to do it that way!"

"I did it that way because your way was wrong and inefficient! As usual!"

"Hey! You seem to be forgetting who's in charge around here and why I'm in charge! I did you a favor by deleting those second-rate docs! You should be on your knees, expressing your gratitude to me!"

"Have you no conscious at all?"

"Don't try to shift the blame here!"

"Are you completely delusional? You *are* to blame! You're *always* to blame!"

"Don't talk to me that way!"

"You're lucky all I'm doing is talking!"

It seemed like an appropriate time to intervene.

"What's going on?" I asked, barging into the office. "I could hear you guys from the elevator."

"Never you mind!" Bradley snapped, shifting his glare from Julian onto me. "I have some bones to pick with you, too!"

Then pick them, Motherfucker! I thought, returning his glare. It was all I could do to keep from kicking his teeth down his throat and out the other end.

"My office, in ten minutes!" he yelled at me, with veins bulging from his temples. Then he stormed out, slamming his office door behind him.

Julian was pacing the room and seething. I'd never seen him remotely angry, let alone in his current state.

"You should sit down for a minute and take some deep breaths," I said, pulling out his desk chair.

"Who the fuck does he think he is?" he growled.

"What the hell happened?"

"Remember the countless, grueling hours I spent preparing those legal documents for Futile Onanist last week? That asshole accessed my computer and deleted every last page *and* the backup copies! Then he had the gall to blame me for not doing it correctly! I can't take it anymore! I could kill him with my bare hands!"

"Whoa!" Finn said, walking in. "What did I miss?"

"Bradley deleted that shitload of work Julian did last week," I replied, keeping my eyes on Julian. "The backup copies, too. Then, as usual, he blamed Julian, for not doing it right, because he didn't do it *his* way."

"Whaaaaaaat? You nearly went postal prepping that shit! *I* could kill him with my bare hands!"

Without saying a word, Julian walked out of our office and over to Bradley's. I wasn't sure if I should follow. After all, Julian was the level-headed one, who always kept his cool, no matter how furious he should have become. He was adept at compartmentalizing business and personal. Besides, he appeared to be in a considerably calmer state than the one I'd found him in. Finn and I stayed put, listening through the walls. I'll never forget the sound that followed: a faint *SPLAT!* Finn and I looked at each other and said, "What the hell was that?" before rushing into Bradley's office.

Julian was standing by the door-sized casement window to the right of Bradley's desk, staring down at the alley. Bradley was nowhere in sight. Finn and I walked over to the window and looked out. There was Bradley on the pavement below, marinating in his own blood and brains. His pants had somehow been pulled down, and his bare ass was sticking straight up in the air. It took every ounce of self-control I had to refrain from laughing. About the bare ass, that is.

"Holy shit!" Finn shrieked, placing his hand over his mouth. *"Did he fucking jump?"* He looked over at Julian. "Or... wait... holy shit!" Then he looked back at Bradley. "Why is his bare ass sticking straight up in the air? Holy shit!"

Julian didn't respond.

I knew exactly what had happened, and my inner criminal instantly switched into damage-control mode. As far as I was concerned, business *was* personal, an incontrovertible truth I'd learned growing up on the streets, where someone like Bradley would have been cut down within five minutes. There was no way in hell Julian was going to prison for ridding the world of that malignant piece of shit. I sat down at Bradley's desk and set back the clock on his computer by one hour. Then I began composing a suicide note, carefully disclosing his crimes, which would serve as the reason for his self-defenestration. Between the computer and bank records, there was plenty of proof, if it ever came to that. Of course, if a forensic investigation was ever done on his laptop, the truth about when the note was written would be revealed, but I couldn't let my mind go there. I needed to work with what I was given. As I typed away, I was unflinchingly focused, as if I were performing surgery that was going to save Julian's life.

"Come on, Brother," Finn said to Julian, directing him away from the window. "Let's sit down."

I sent the finished document to the printer, pulled it out, and quickly looked it over before handing it to Finn. "So, what do you think?" I asked, giving him a moment to read it.

"It's fucking perfect!" he exclaimed. "Jesus, how the hell did you write that so damn fast? I'm totally freaking out here."

"I'm more freaked out by the prospect of us going to prison," I said, taking the note from him. "We need to get our shit together before calling the cops."

"Okay, I'm working on it," he said, inhaling and exhaling. "Deep breaths… deep breaths…"

I placed the note on Bradley's desk, reset the clock on his computer, and walked over to Julian. "Julian?" I said, staring into his glazed eyes. "Are you listening?"

"Yes, I'm listening," he said, nodding.

"You're not going to prison, do you hear me?"

"Yeah, Dude," Finn added. "No fucking way that's happening. I don't care what your pesky conscience is saying. Tell it to shut the fuck up. We're gonna tell the cops that Bradley jumped. Do you follow?"

"Yes, I follow," Julian replied coolly. "One of us needs to call the police. *Now*."

"I'm on it," I said, picking up Bradley's phone and dialing. "Be quiet for a minute."

When the dispatcher answered, I told her, in a feigned frantic voice, that my boss had jumped out of his tenth-floor window. She asked if he was alive. I told her I was calling from his office and couldn't tell, but was heading down there after hanging up with her. Then I asked her to send an ambulance, stat. She confirmed the address and said help was on its way.

"Okay, now we need to get our story straight and fast," I said to my partners in crime. "They're going to be here any minute."

"Are you sure you're all right?" Finn asked Julian.

"Yes, I'm fine," Julian replied firmly.

"Because she and I can do all the talking, and tell the cops you're in shock because you just saw Bradley jump. Or... wait... *did* you see him jump? Did any of us see him jump? Shit! I'm a scene! Maybe *I* shouldn't do *any* of the talking!"

"None of us saw him jump," I said, hearing sirens approaching in the distance. "That will make our story simpler and more consistent. If the cops start asking for details, we don't need to be contradicting each other."

"Did we *hear* him jump, then? Or hit the ground?" Finn asked, peering out the window. "Shit, I hope no one *did* see or hear anything!"

"I seriously doubt anyone saw or heard it," I said, looking down at the alley. "Someone would be down there by now. Thank god it was that window and not one of the others."

"It would have been impossible for any of us to have seen or heard *anything* from our office," Julian interjected, standing up. "*Especially* with our windows and Bradley's door closed, which are crucial details to remember when speaking to the police, I might add." Then he paused for a moment and continued, "Okay, here's the story: I went to Bradley's office to get some papers signed. When I knocked on the door, he didn't answer, so I entered and didn't see him sitting at his desk. Then I called you guys in, and after pondering his whereabouts for a couple of minutes, I looked out the window and saw him lying in the alley. Now we need to get ourselves down there before the police and paramedics arrive. It's 10:22, by the way. When they ask what time I went to his office to get those papers signed, tell them 10:15."

Finn and I assented. Then the three of us made a dash for the elevator, as discreetly as possible.

I'd seen a dead body before, as a child, when one of the neighborhood kids, Jimmy Clayton, had been hit by a Winnebago while riding his bike. As gruesome as that was, it didn't come close to the mangled mess that lay before me. I expected to feel a measure of contrition or perhaps sympathy, but instead, I was overcome with the most exquisite sense of relief.

Julian knelt beside the corpse and flipped it over.

"Dude, don't touch him!" Finn exclaimed, shaking his hands squeamishly.

"One of us has to," Julian replied, leaning over Bradley's mutilated face and checking for a pulse. "It'll look suspicious if no one checks to see if he's alive."

"Plus, it's best if he's not found in the position in which he landed," I added. "If the crime scene is intact, it'll make it much easier for them to perform a proper investigation, which means they may figure out that it wasn't a suicide."

"Good point," Finn said, looking down at Bradley's exposed and diminutive manhood. "Is someone going to pull up his pants, or what? I think I'm going to puke or crack up... or both... in no particular order."

Julian stood up and assessed the situation. Then he squatted beside the corpse and carefully pulled up the pants, leaving the button and zipper open. "That's good enough," he said, getting to his feet. "I don't want to mess with him too much."

When the police arrived, they wasted no time in launching into the inevitable interrogation. Luckily, they questioned all three of us at once, right there at the scene. Julian did most of the talking and was so convincing even *I* bought it, forgetting for a moment that a murder had been committed. *Who knew he had it in him?* When the investigators swept Bradley's office, they found the note, which prompted another round of questions. All three of us acknowledged seeing the note *after* he had jumped, acting as though his reasons for whacking himself came as a complete shock. Our performances throughout were award-worthy. Finn and I even managed to conjure up some fake tears. The cops kept us there for three tense hours. Then my blood brothers and I headed to Finn's apartment to discuss the day's events and our future plans. Okay, I'll admit there was some celebration involved, and not merely because we had gotten away with murder. While some may disagree with how it was done, wiping a festering pustule like Bradley off the face of the earth was an act of mercy. The man was a sociopathic tyrant who psychologically massacred those closest to him. Even his 14-year-old twin daughters, who he treated like doodads, would be better off without him, especially given his perverse tendencies. As for Belinda, she was decidedly more devastated by the fact that she had been married to a pedophile who was having an affair with her underage niece than the unexpected suicide. I got the distinct feeling she knew there was more to the already lurid story, but didn't want to spoil the glorious denouement by learning the truth. She knew better than anyone that Bradley would take the lives of a million others, including hers and their children's, before taking his own.

One month after the auspicious incident, Julian, Finn, and I reopened shop, with Belinda's blessings. Not as employees, but as equal partners. With every last drop of poison squeezed out, the business began to thrive as it did when Belinda's old man was in charge. Julian also signed a handful of quality acts to counterbalance the likes of Futile Onanist & The Flaccid Putz, sealing our reputation as a respectable yet cutting-edge firm.

As it turned out, Belinda had some brilliant ideas that Bradley had foolishly shot down simply because they weren't his own. Remember when I said she had untapped potential? Well, it came to the surface and shined. Having finally found her place in the present, she began inching her way out of the cage of her past and eventually rarely returned.

MIASMA OF MENDACITY

She appeared to be good-natured, interesting, and highly intelligent, but her expressionless eyes told a darker, more insidious tale. Soon after entering the circle, she began dishing out gratuitous opinions, unwarranted brickbats, and transparent smarm — the recipients of each dependent on her ulterior motives. Her proclivity for ejaculating painfully longwinded displays of her vast knowledge, while bragging about her numerous talents and achievements became increasingly grating, but was soon offset by the revelation that her {Insert Loved One} had suffered an unspecified tragic demise. Encouraged and mildly intoxicated by the response it garnered, she began using the grievous blow in an extortionate manner, to elicit sympathy and tolerance, thus "excusing" any inexcusable behavior. Then came the tales of sexual harassment and abuse, and various health issues — always told in elaborate detail, yet inconsistent and contradictory. Although there were semblances of truth, the whole production carried a miasma of mendacity that went carelessly unnoticed, until it was too late. By the time the toxic stench had permeated the circle, she had embedded herself like a black-legged tick. Extraction was nearly impossible, and no one could have predicted the carnage that would be left in her wake.

Who is she, you ask? If you've spent any time on social networking sites, you've likely encountered a watered-down and more innocuous version of her. The internet can connect kindred souls who might have never met otherwise. It can also engender, perpetuate, and exacerbate pathological behaviors that might have never materialized in what's naively referred to as "the real world." Among those behaviors are factitious disorders and factitious disorders by proxy, both of which have been given a fresh twist with the advent of the online forum. Arguably, one of the primary reasons for being on a social networking site is to solicit and hopefully receive attention, approval, and love. As with other activities that can provide instant gratification, social networking can become addictive. Some people get hooked on the attention gained from sharing good news, which can morph into a form of positive-reinforcement, while others get hooked on sympathy-driven attention, which can drive them to exaggerate or lie about their adversities. In the case of the woman I'm speaking of, she became so dependent on the latter it drove her to do the unthinkable.

It was a mystery how she came upon the circle, which consisted of like-minded creative people located across the globe. Everyone took it for granted that someone else knew her, and no one bothered to find out if anyone knew her at all. In the bubble of social media, superficial criteria, such as common interests and the number of mutual friends, is used to determine whether someone is worthy of "friending." Since most people either falsify information on their profiles or exclude it altogether, there isn't much else to go by anyway. It's a leap in the dark, and as I mentioned, the woman's facade was quite impressive. So much so, I think people *wanted* her to be what she claimed to be, which is probably why they took her gloss as gospel. My first interaction with her occurred in a discussion about 'Pataphysics. I was instantly taken by her sharp wit and frightening intellect. After exchanging some dialogue in that thread, I received a friend request, which I accepted without hesitation. Noticing she was already friends with a handful of people in the circle, I connected her with all the others, since she was too delightful not to share.

She remained delightful for a month, before her true personality reared its maladjusted head. It began with a profusion of ingratiating praise for some and undeserved disparagement for others, depending on their gender, age, achievements, utility, and how much attention they gave her. She decidedly favored men of all ages over women who were younger and more attractive than her, and automatically classified the latter as mentally inferior, even if they weren't. Her intellect – which was initially charming – became an irritant when she began using it in a condescending manner. Her sole purpose for participating in threads was to dominate. Regardless of the topic, she invariably found a way to make herself the center of attention. Realizing she wasn't as stable as they had originally thought, people in the circle began to withdraw. She must have sensed she was losing them, because there was no other explanation for what happened next. In a complete departure from her usual posturing, she revealed, via a poignantly written post, that not only had her husband died of cancer, but that she herself was a three-time cancer survivor. If that weren't tragic enough, she had also been rendered barren after her first and only child was stillborn. With that single post, all transgressions were instantly forgiven. It was no wonder she was a little off, and how could anyone be intolerant of someone who had endured such trials? More heartrending revelations followed, including the sudden and untimely deaths of her dearest friends, numerous instances of sexual harassment, and a brutal rape that had happened while she was walking home from the bus stop one night. Any antipathy toward her came to an abrupt halt, and the level of interaction on her profile increased significantly. People couldn't sympathize enough, posting volumes of comments to show their support. She appeared to be in her glory, gorging herself on the feast of attention. I sat back and observed, *knowing* there was more than met the eye.

The social networking site was like a formicarium. If you spent enough time on it, the patterns became glaringly obvious. Most members had short attention spans and grew bored easily, as they did with her martyrly song and dance after a couple of weeks. She carried on desperately for several more days, but everyone had lost interest. That was when she stepped up her sick game. First, she posted a melodramatic and intentionally vague announcement, stating she had personal matters to deal with and would be leaving the site indefinitely. Then she deactivated her account. A week later, she reappeared and announced that her "beloved mother" had died. People who didn't know her beyond the site – which seemed to account for her entire roster – didn't ask for details, and she didn't offer any. As expected, there was an outpouring of condolences, which she lapped up as quickly as they were dispensed. It continued for a couple of weeks, before everyone moved on again. A failed attempt at further milking the tragedy was followed by another post about more personal matters to tend to, followed by another deactivation. A week later, she reappeared with the heartbreaking news that her father had died. *Both parents dead within a month?* Everyone was feeling her sorrow, beneath a measure of skepticism, since she didn't appear to be feeling much sorrow herself. I resisted my nagging temptation to inquire about what had happened to her parents. Perhaps they had been gravely ill for ages and their passing was a blessing? Or perhaps they were monsters who had abused her as a child? Perhaps that was why she came across as blissed out rather than broken? I only knew that her enthusiastic reaction to the spate of sympathy was suspicious. She seemed to be enjoying it far too much for someone who claimed to be grieving.

Her father's death earned her two more weeks of attention, before everyone moved on again, causing her to become even more temperamental. She would begin each day with her usual platitudinous morning affirmation, only now there were tinges of cynicism and morbidity. That lunacy would be followed by a deluge of the most outrageous and depressing news stories imaginable, with which she would drown her so-called friends, like a bizarre form of displacement. She would cap off the day with a melancholy song, accompanied by one of her trite and maudlin poems. People expressed concern among themselves, but were not concerned enough to take action. Perhaps if they had, some lives could have been saved.

The ritual continued for three weeks, until it was interrupted by the inconceivable news that not only had her sister died, but her brother as well. Her entire immediate family was now gone. How was that even possible? As with her parents, she kept their causes of death under wraps, claiming to be "too devastated to talk about it" whenever anyone attempted to ask. Of course, everyone in the circle was worried about her safety and wellbeing. Besides the fact that it was more loss than *anyone* should be dealt in such a short time period, it was as though her family had been cursed. Or maybe they had a price on their heads? Would she be next? After all, her background was a closed book.

The poor woman was showered with condolences and support, but when the level of interaction on her profile fizzled out, her agitation became palpable. She began lashing out, without the slightest provocation, while threatening repeatedly to leave the site for good. Everyone attributed it to massive bereavement, and opted to give her space rather than consolation, which only further enraged her. I figured she would at least deactivate again, if for no other reason than to make people worry about whether she would return. The worrying part would only exist in her imagination, since it was common for members to vanish from the site for days, even weeks at a time without anyone noticing. Instead of casting that stale and predictable cloud of concern, she maneuvered in an unforeseen direction that would change the lives of everyone in the circle.

As I mentioned, she favored men, especially those whose intellect was on a par with hers. Shortly after entering the circle, she had latched on to one man in particular, with her avid interest in him bordering on cyberstalking. They chatted on the social networking site on a daily sometimes hourly basis and had even exchanged care packages in the mail. Enamored by her extraordinary mind, the man was flattered at first, but soon began to feel claustrophobic. Along with her insatiable appetite for attention, the woman would project onto him what she wanted him to be, going so far as to believe that he had intense romantic feelings for her, which was not remotely true. To begin with, he was happily married. While the woman's behavior was unsettling, the man felt sorry for her, especially after she had lost her entire family. He could never bring himself to shut her out completely, but would often deactivate his profile on the site so she couldn't reach him. He also set up filters on his email accounts. He figured she was ultimately harmless, and that any potential harassment would be confined to the virtual world. If only that were the case.

During one of those avoidance deactivations, the woman struck up a conversation with the man's wife, who had forgotten to disable the site's chat feature that morning. It began with a paranoid interrogation about the man's whereabouts, before mushrooming into a prolonged discussion on literature and politics, with the wife reluctantly participating out of sympathy. An hour into it, the woman blurted out that she had taken an overdose of sleeping pills, claiming that with her family gone, she had no reason to live. Then she ended the chat. Shocked, the wife searched the internet for the number of the police department in the woman's podunk town. When someone answered on the other end, the wife explained the improbable situation and gave the confused officer the woman's address, which was written on a sticky note affixed to the refrigerator. Thankfully, he took the call seriously and dispatched a squad car to the woman's home, assuring the wife he would keep her posted. Two hours later, the wife got word that the woman was alive and safe. It turned out she hadn't taken any pills, let alone an entire bottle, but her stunt was viewed as an attempt, which, according to the law, warranted an involuntarily psychiatric hold. It would not be her first, far from it.

Two weeks after the suicide scare, the wife sent the woman a brief message to see how she was doing. The woman answered merely seconds after the wife had pressed the "Send" button. The wife thought it weird, but what wasn't weird about the woman. After insisting she was "back to her usual self," the woman broached a subject that made the wife's ears perk up.

She wanted to meet in person. She happened to be in town, and although the coincidence was suspect, the wife's curiosity was beyond piqued. Everyone in the circle had been dying to meet the woman in the flesh, simply to see if she was real, but it seemed as though an opportunity would never present itself. The wife's husband was out of town – which the woman seemed oddly glad to hear – but there was no reason the two ladies couldn't meet for lunch at the woman's hotel. Now would be a good time, I suppose, to let you know that *I* am the man's wife.

When I arrived at the restaurant, the following day, the woman was nowhere in sight. I wasn't surprised, but wanted to give her the benefit of the doubt. Perhaps she was merely running late?

"Your companion hasn't arrived yet," the hostess said, showing me to the table. "Can I bring you a drink while you wait?"

"I'm sure she'll be here soon," I said, preoccupied with the possibility of her being a no-show. "A glass of ice water would be wonderful, thank you."

After waiting for 25 minutes, I walked over to the front desk to see if a message had been left. If she was indeed in that hotel, I was not going anywhere until I saw her. "Excuse me," I asked the concierge, "I was wondering…" Before I could finish, my phone rang. It was the woman, with a change of plans.

"Hi!" she said in a pleasant voice. "I am so sorry! Please accept my deepest apologies. I was caught on a business call and could not get away."

"That's okay," I lied, analyzing the sound of her voice, which I'd never heard before.

"I feel terrible!" she continued, as though I hadn't said a word. "The person I was talking to is notorious for rambling on and not letting anyone get one word in edgewise."

Sounds like someone I know, I laughed to myself.

"We can reschedule, if you're too busy?" I said, hoping she would say no.

"I wouldn't dream of it! You know, the balcony in my suite here is so beautiful and spacious, why don't we order in and dine there instead? It would give us more privacy as well."

I would have agreed to meet her in a fetid garbage bin at that point. "That sounds nice. What's your room number?"

"Twenty-three. It's at the end of the hall, to your right. I'll see you in a couple of minutes. Ciao!"

I headed to the elevator, purchasing a bouquet of flowers from the gift shop along the way. It would be rude to show up empty-handed.

When the elevator doors opened, the woman was standing there. I took a moment to check her out as discreetly as possible. She was much more petite and mature looking in person than in her photos.

"Hello!" she said, embracing me tightly. "Wow! It is so wonderful to finally meet you!"

"You as well," I said, finding her hug too forceful for comfort.

"I apologize again for keeping you waiting," she laughed. "I want to murder people who are late!"

"Here, these are for you," I said, handing her the fragrant bouquet.

"Oh, wow, thank you!" she said, smiling warmly. "They're lovely!"

"My pleasure," I said, returning her smile.

"Well, shall we?" she said, placing her left hand on my back and leading me down the hallway.

Seconds after the door had closed, I was blindsided, struck on the back of the head with a blunt object. As soon as I hit the ground, face first, the woman pounced on me, pulled back my head, and stuffed a ball gag into my mouth. *"Don't you dare yell for help,"* she warned, tightening the strap. I was stunned, physically and mentally. Before I could even think about defending myself, she delivered another blow that knocked me out cold.

When I regained consciousness, a half-hour later, I was bound to the bed, spread eagle and stark naked. Even more disturbing, the woman was performing cunnilingus on me, aggressively shoving her tongue in and out of my vagina, while giving my clitoris a deep lick with each thrust. Most disturbing of all, I couldn't help being *physically* aroused, even though I was repulsed and horrified. I attempted to free myself from the binds and scream for help, but it was no use.

Realizing I was awake, she stopped and came up for air. "Mmmmm, you sure are sweet," she moaned, going back down. "Are you going to cum?"

Struggling to switch off all sensation, I felt myself climaxing against my will.

She slid up to my chest and began massaging my breasts with her left hand, while shoving the forefinger of her right hand into my vagina. "Ooh, look how wet you are!" she squealed with a wicked smile. "You *loved* that, didn't you!"

It was too surreal and sickening to process. Every woman fears being raped, but I *never* imagined it could come at the hands of a woman. I didn't even know it was possible.

"Wait until you see what I have for you next!" she laughed, peeling off her black silk robe as she pranced out of the room.

I kept my eyes on her, wishing I could unsee the sight of her naked body. Her ass was flat, wrinkly, and bony, like a 100-year-old man's. The instant she turned the corner, I made another attempt at freeing myself, but the binds were too tight. She returned moments later, wearing the creepiest latex doll mask imaginable and a cartoonishly giant flesh-colored strap-on dildo. "It's double-sided," she purred, sashaying toward the bed, while fondling her sagging breasts. If it hadn't been such a grotesquely alarming vision, it would have been absurd, even hilarious. For the next three hours, she raped me repeatedly, forcing me to orgasm over and over again, despite strenuous efforts to remain numb. I was incapacitated by the physical, mental, and emotional trauma. After the final assault, she removed the gear, planted herself on my stomach, and spilled the whole story about her family. They were indeed dead, and *she* had murdered them all, with a rare and undetectable poison. Her reason? So she could post about their deaths on the social networking site in exchange for attention. She confessed to being hooked on the sympathy-driven variety, saying it began in childhood, when she would slaughter the family pets to feed her implacable addiction. It progressed into adulthood, with the killings of a number of friends and boyfriends, as well as her husband, who never had *any* kind of cancer. Not surprisingly, neither had she. Most startlingly, her child had not been stillborn, but rather smothered as a newborn while sleeping in his crib.

"I suffer from Munchausen Syndrome By Proxy," she confessed confidently, as though it were a source of pride. "I've been under psychiatric care for most of my life, and have spent time in some of our country's most reputable institutions."

It obviously hasn't helped, I thought, *and why the hell did they let her out?*

"The internet has breathed new life into me!" she continued, with a maniacal look in her eyes. "With its infinite audience at my fingertips, the possibilities are limitless! My life-affirming cacoethes can thrive more than I had ever hoped!"

I stared at her while she rhapsodized, petrified by what she might do next.

"Well, I had a divine time, my dear," she hissed, wiping the sweat from my brow. "I must say, it was far more delightful than having an ordinary old meal with you and your husband, who I still intend to see. When I learned you were coming alone, I could hardly contain myself. You see, I've fantasized about raping a strong woman for as long as I can remember. I thought

I would never be able to check that off my bucket list, and for that, I thank you profusely."

I held my stare.

"Now, you know I can't possibly let you live," she continued, matter-of-factly, "but I assure you, your death will be as painless as possible."

Disgusted by the sight of her, I closed my eyes for a moment before resuming my stare.

"Your husband's death too," she added in a smug tone. "After I tire of him, that is."

When those words crossed her cracked lips, my stare turned into a glare and my fear turned into rage. I was determined to break free and hurt, if not kill, the psychotic bitch.

"Hmmmm, I need to figure out how to dispose of your body," she said contemplatively, as though she were planning the lunch menu. "I think I can squeeze you into my Louis Vuitton Zephyr 70, if I break your limbs first."

I was now foaming at the mouth, but needed to conserve my energy and remain focused, if I expected to extricate myself from the fix I'd gotten myself into and settle the score.

"I'll work it all out in a nice hot bath," she yawned, getting up. "Now, don't you dare go anywhere, my dear!" she laughed fiendishly. "I'll be right back!"

I waited until I heard the bathroom door close before making my move. During the third hour of the assault, I'd noticed that the bind on my right hand had loosened ever so slightly. Freeing that hand was my only hope. I wriggled and yanked until I broke skin and bled, then wriggled, yanked, and bled some more. Five minutes later, my hand was free. After untying the other binds, I removed the ball gag and put on the silk robe she had left on the floor. Then I searched the bedroom for a suitable weapon. All I could find was a metal nail file on the nightstand. Not my first choice, but it would have to do. I had at least seven inches of height and 20 pounds on the woman, which meant I should be able to take her with relative ease. If she hadn't bushwhacked me, she never would have gotten the upper hand in the first place. Why didn't I call or go for help, you ask? Retribution was the only cure for the damage, pain, and humiliation the crazy cunt had caused. I'd never be able to move on without at least returning a portion of what I'd been given. Those film scenes in which the protagonist has the villain's life in his hands and opts to let the law deliver justice instead? Unqualified bullshit.

I tiptoed over to the bathroom and put my ear up against the door. She was singing out loud, but I didn't hear any music. Was she listening to an MP3 player? If so, my edge would be that much sharper. Of course, the bathroom's layout was completely unknown, and I would only have a moment to survey it after opening the door. The singing abruptly stopped. *Shit*, I thought. *Maybe I should return to the bedroom and ambush her? Or I could get her when she comes out of the bathroom?* Before I could decide, she let out a resounding groan. Without giving it another thought, I flung open the door and charged in, only to be met by the most atrocious odor. I quickly scanned the room – which was the size of a master bedroom – and spotted her in the corner, on the toilet taking a dump. After locking eyes for a split second, she jumped to her feet and came at me, with runny feces spilling out of her ass. I certainly wasn't going to just stand there and wait for her to reach me. Before I could take a single step, she slipped on her own shit and fell back, hitting her head on the stone floor. She convulsed for half a minute then froze, as a trickle of blood seeped out from under her skull. *It couldn't be that simple, could it?* I checked her pulse and began to cachinnate, despite myself. Besides the fact that her fall was unintentional comedic brilliance – not to mention the poetic justice of her own shit leading to her ruination – she was dead, and I didn't have to lay one finger on her.

Leaving the psychopath lying in her mephitic and unlikely bane, I searched for my purse, which I found in the bedroom closet. I pulled out my phone only to discover that the battery had been removed. *Naturally,* I thought. Fearing the madwoman might not be dead, or *might be undead*, I rushed out into the hallway and screamed for help.

A man in the adjacent room came out right away, with a phone in his hand, conveniently. "What in god's name is going on out here?" he asked.

"Call 911!" I yelled repeatedly. "I was kidnapped and raped!"

The man looked at me in disbelief.

"Call 911!" I yelled once more, coming at him, fully intending to grab the phone from his hand if he didn't cooperate.

Understandably taken aback, he halted me with his free hand and began dialing with the other. "Okay, okay, just calm down! I'm calling now!"

As soon as the call was made, the man asked if I was injured. I responded by telling him exactly what had happened in that hotel room, knowing it would not only sound implausible, but ridiculous. After all, women didn't rape other women, right?

The hotel security team arrived moments later, and the police, moments after that. When I told them I'd been knocked unconscious and sexually assaulted, they called for an ambulance. I was taken to a nearby hospital, where two marshals and the woman's shrink were awaiting my arrival. Before making a statement about my own ordeal, I told them about every murder to which the woman had confessed. It turned out the authorities had been looking for her for days. After her mandatory stint in the booby hatch, she had been remanded to a halfway house for psychiatric patients, where she was to remain for a period of one year. A week and a half into her sentence, she had escaped and caught an airplane to the city where my husband and I live. I suspect her original plan was to assault, torture and whack me, and then live out her fantasy with him, but I'll never know.

By the following weekend, I had returned to my usual routine, including whiling away several hours a day on the social networking site. Although I was the only real victim from the circle, they were all profoundly and permanently affected, as if they had been in that hotel room with me. It was enough to make a handful of them leave the site for good, my husband among them. It was eerie to see the woman's profile still active. I wondered if it would remain active, or if some legal authority would eventually shut it down. I don't know why, but I haven't unfriended her.

RESIPISCENT RECIDIVIST

Karen was killed instantly, when her Audi slammed head-on into the eucalyptus trees, before rolling over the median and into oncoming traffic. The passenger fractured half the bones in her body, suffered a brain injury, and spent several months in a coma, ultimately emerging as an eidolon. It was a predestined tragedy that had been set into motion seven years prior, when grasping long division should have been Karen's main concern.

As a child, Karen was learning disabled and spoke with an impediment, making her the butt of ridicule. *"She's a retard and she talks funny!"* her classmates would tease incessantly. Over time, the rhythmic doses of derisive poison saturated Karen's psyche, driving her to retaliate. Rather than unleashing her righteous anger on her tormentors, she misplaced it onto the meek and vulnerable, as is often the case. With her abuse toward one child in particular, Karen had unknowingly sealed her own violent and untimely demise. While bullying is fairly common among children, her chosen target was not a common child, which neither Karen nor the child knew at the time.

It all began with the theft of a coveted wristwatch. According to the student body at Karen's school, these grail-like timepieces were as compulsory as the three Rs. Like every other fad that had preceded and would follow, anyone who didn't buy into the worth-defining trend was labeled a "no one." Despite her cognitive deficit, Karen's materialistic nature and need to fit in rivaled her peers'. She couldn't keep up with Math or English, but when it came to keeping up with the mini Joneses and being a "someone," she was as hungry as the next kid. Although her parents were well-off and could easily afford to buy a dozen watches, like every must-have item, the stores couldn't keep them in stock. That wasn't going to stop Karen. An opportunity to steal one presented itself the day before her birthday. For weeks, she had been stalking a classmate whose watch she wanted. It was purple, with her favorite cartoon character on its face. Before playing tetherball during recess each morning, the owner of the watch would remove it and place it on a picnic table nearby. On that particular day, the girl accidently left it behind when returning to class. Lurking behind a tree on the sidelines, Karen swooped down and stuffed the watch into her pocket.

By lunchtime, news of the crime had spread across the school, propelling Karen's paranoia into overdrive. She had to hide the loot, and fast. Her first and only thought was to force another kid to take possession of the watch until the heat died down. It was here that the ominous seed was planted. The chosen target, who Karen had barely noticed before, had the misfortune of being alone in the girls' restroom when Karen came storming in. Unbeknown to Karen, targeting that child would be the most momentous, not to mention fatal, decision she would ever make.

"Take this and hide it somewhere good, where no one will find it!" Karen yelled, cornering the child and shoving the wristwatch into her hands. "If you say one word about it to anyone, I'll beat you up so bad!"

"Why?" the child asked, startled and confused. "Is that the stolen watch everyone's talking about?"

Her question was met with a shove that knocked her to the ground.

"Just shut up and do what I say!" Karen growled, standing over the child with one foot on her stomach. "Take it and hide it somewhere good, and don't tell anyone I gave it to you!"

Being the chronic new kid, the child was used to being picked on and knew her defensive limitations. Karen was, in fact, a sixth grader who had been held back two years, which meant she was bigger and stronger than most of the *boys* in the school, never mind the girls. That disadvantage, combined with the child's increasingly volatile home life – which had crushed her fighting spirit – gave her no choice but to buckle. "Okay," she mumbled, stuffing the watch into her pants pocket. "How long do I have to keep it?"

"For as long as I say, Retard!" Karen snapped, with a psychotic glare that obliterated the child's remaining traces of courage. Then she yanked the lunchbox from the child's trembling hands and stormed out as quickly as she had stormed in.

The child waited ten minutes before getting up, and another ten minutes before leaving the scene. By then, lunch was over. As she exited the restroom, she spotted her beloved Snoopy lunchbox in the garbage can outside the door. Heaving a deep sigh, she pulled it out. It was covered with muck and riddled with dents, as though it had been mercilessly stomped on. Realizing its contents had been emptied as well, she heaved another sigh, deeper than the first. As the bell rang, she trudged back into the restroom to restore the lunchbox's dignity the best she could.

When the child arrived home that afternoon, the key wasn't where it was supposed to be, under the fake rock near the creepy, weather-beaten garden gnomes. Her mother must have forgotten again. It was the third time in as many weeks. When the child's father had moved out in December, her mother claimed to be on the road to recovery, which was far from true. She was not only popping more pills than ever, but had started drinking as well. Her 12-Stepping father was no better, considering he had left his young daughter in the care of someone who was precariously unstable. His denial and self-righteousness might have made him worse. While the child loved her parents and believed they loved her, they were both disgracefully unfit and had no business bringing her into the world. Pondering that undeniable truth for the billionth time, she sat down and leaned against the front door, wincing in excruciating pain. She placed her hand on her lower back and winced again. It was a contusion caused by

Karen's assault, and a sizable one at that. Her tailbone ached too, like it had after she had been kicked by one of the neighborhood boys last year. No wonder it had been so difficult to sit and walk from lunch onward. The child got to her feet and headed to the backyard. She always left her bedroom window ajar, and could probably squeeze through with some effort. As she passed through the gate, her stomach began to cramp. Thanks to her mother's gestational drug use, the child had been born with severe gastrointestinal problems that continued to plague her in spurts, especially when she was distressed. Once an attack was underway, it was impossible to keep it from running its course, which meant sudden and unstoppable defecation. The child ran frantically toward the bushes near the back fence, not having the luxury of worrying about toilet paper. After cleaning herself with some leaves, she took a couple of minutes to soak in the euphoric relief that invariably followed the voiding of excrement. She couldn't understand how a bodily function that was supposed to be natural could cause such agony. Looking across the yard, she spotted the neighbor's orange tomcat taking a dump near the snapdragons. He didn't appear to be in any discomfort at all. *Must be nice,* the child thought. Taking a cue from him, she covered her feces with dirt. Then she went to check the bedroom window, which, much to her frustration was not only closed, but locked. Her mother, again. *"Figures,"* the child whispered to herself. Calling her negligent father would be pointless, and her mother wouldn't be home until seven, which meant the child would have to wait outside until then. Having gone without lunch, she was starving, and it was making her injured back throb even more. She removed her hoodie, draped it on the overgrown grass under the jacaranda tree, and reclined. As the heliotrope flowers rained down, she dreamed about running away with The Marx Brothers.

In the days following the assault, Karen threatened and roughed up the child at every opportunity, reminding her of the mortal beating that would come if she sang. The child thought it impossible to loathe school more than she already did, but Karen proved her wrong. While it had always been hellish, the stress caused by Karen's mounting brutality now made it unbearable. Along with a number of other compulsive behaviors, the child's parents were moving junkies. During their infinite relocations, the child had become adept at feigning illness in order to avoid school. She saw no better time than the present to utilize that skill until she graduated high school, since Karen's reign of terror would likely continue for at least that long.

The child implemented her plan on Monday, but it only worked until Sunday, when her mother happened upon the watch while cleaning the child's room.

"Where did you get this wristwatch?" her mother asked, knowing the child couldn't have purchased the ridiculously overpriced timepiece.

Hearing Karen's threats echoing in her head, the child was silent.

"Did you find it?" her mother asked sternly.

"No," the child replied, struggling to maintain her composure.

"Did you steal it?"

"No!"

"How did you get it, then? Whose is it?"

"It's mine," the child lied. "Suzy gave it to me."

"Suzy? What for?"

"She said it was a present for being her friend."

"That's an extremely expensive gift," her mother said, shaking her head. "You shouldn't have accepted it. I'm going to call her mother and tell her it's too much."

"No! Don't do that!" the child cried out.

"Why not?"

"Because Suzy didn't give it to me."

"Okay, now you've lost me," her mother laughed. "Tell me where you got the watch."

The child didn't respond.

"All right," her mother sighed. "I'm going to call your teacher tomorrow to see if she knows anything about it. I have a funny feeling someone at your school is missing a watch."

That was the child's breaking point. She would not only be unjustly accused of stealing the watch, but also subjected to Karen's abuse for the rest of her life. She would be a pariah *and* punching bag. Bursting into tears, the child spilled the entire story, emphasizing her intense fear of what Karen would do, while begging her mother for mercy. Undeterred by the desperate pleas, her mother insisted on reporting both the theft and assault the following morning. The child believed her death warrant had been signed.

"You did the right thing by telling me," her mother said, giving the child a hug. "I promise you won't be punished by anyone, including this girl Karen."

The child didn't believe her.

On Tuesday, there was a meeting between the child, the child's mother, the principal, Karen's parents, and much to Karen's dismay, Karen herself. Of course, she vehemently denied the charges, pointing her spiteful finger at the child and presenting herself as a lamb.

"*She* stole it! *She* stole it!" Karen cried over and over again. "It was *her, her, her,* not me!"

No one bought it for a moment, not even Karen's parents. Apparently, their daughter had a proclivity for stealing whatever they couldn't or wouldn't give her. It was also apparent that discipline was dispensed sparingly in their household, which would explain Karen's sociopathic sense of entitlement. The meeting concluded with a three-day suspension for Karen and brownie points for the child for her role as scapegoat, which only intensified Karen's rage.

For the next several weeks, Karen vowed to get revenge on the child, promising to deliver a thrashing of ferocious proportions. Threats, menacing looks, and obscene hand gestures were as far as it went, though. That was more than enough for the child, now trapped in a perpetual state of crippling anxiety, even when sleeping. All she could do was wish that her mother would be struck with the impulse to move again. It wasn't as if the child would be leaving behind any real friends. The constant relocations made it impossible to form solid relationships. Yes, the only solution was to move, and hopefully, to another planet. As luck would have it, a variation of that wish would soon be granted.

In May, the child and her classmates learned that their school would be closing at the end of the year. Come September, the students would be attending new elementary schools within the district, determined by their home addresses. For the child, it was like being transferred from San Quentin to Taft. Although she still had eight years left to serve in her mandatory educational sentence, she would finally be rid of her tormentor, who would be sent to a school on the other end of town. Since they lived on opposite sides of the tracks, the chances of them running into each other outside of school were slim. The child had never been so relieved. All she had to do was make it through the next month. Well aware of their impending separation, Karen upped her sadistic game, making torturing the child her number one priority.

Although it doesn't seem that way at the time, the years of childhood slip by at the same pace as every other year in a human life. It wasn't long before Karen and the child wound up at the same middle school, which was now the only middle school in their tiny, insular city. The child was understandably concerned, but in the time since their last encounter, Karen had rejected her brutish ways in favor of amity. For reasons unknown, she had been granted admission into the popular circle, thus relinquishing her role as "the retard who talks funny." The "worthiness" gauge of children and adolescents may be harsher and more complex than that of adults — which only refutes the preposterous idea that human beings are basically good. Coming out on the favorable side of the perverse evaluation helped Karen develop into a decent young lady who seemed incapable of being a bully, let alone a thief. She was nice to everyone, including the child, although the child remained on guard. Having moved from a fish bowl into a pond, she was now the target of a gang of bullies — all girls, like Karen, from affluent families. The pattern simply couldn't be ignored, and the child couldn't help wondering how people who were so blessed could be so steeped in inherent cruelty. It seemed to her that if one were wanting for fuck all, and always had been, one would be genial by nature, or at the very least, innocuous. While her tormentors focused on their wardrobes, earning high marks, and participating in extracurricular activities, the child's sole aim was to survive.

Thankfully, the three years of middle school flew by, each at a faster pace than the previous. The child, now a troubled and misanthropic teenager, was riding out the final four years of her stretch in a compulsory educational environment, albeit barely. High school proved to be more hellish than all of the other clinks, combined. The upside was that it was much easier to ditch, which the child did on a regular basis. As for Karen, she was an exemplary member of the student body. Loved by her teachers and peers alike, she excelled scholastically and personally. Even the child couldn't help liking the reformed beast who had once dominated her every thought. Although they never became friends, Karen always treated her with kindness when they passed each other in the hallways. There was not a drop of bad blood between them, and the child found it difficult to imagine that such a vicious and despicable creature had ever existed beneath that warm smile.

It mattered not, for despite it all, the ominous seed, which had been planted all those years ago, had been burgeoning *with a vengeance*. It existed to remember Karen's inhumanity, and when the moment was right, deliver a brand of justice to which society would be oblivious. When Karen was struck down on that fateful night, the entire city went into mourning, believing it was a preventable accident caused by her propensity for speeding and that treacherous stretch of the road. The child believed the same, not knowing that she was involuntarily to blame. Karen's untimely demise was, in fact, a case of preordained retribution, driven by a preternatural force present in chosen individuals, often without their knowledge. Vengeance is automatically set into motion by others' wrongdoings against such individuals, who rarely wish for it. The act itself can occur within minutes, hours, days, months, years, even decades, and doesn't always result in death. Its timing, course, and severity are dictated by the same force, which again, is beyond the control of those who possess it. No, the child Karen had impetuously targeted in that school restroom, on that long-ago afternoon, was *not* a common child.

As for the passenger in Karen's car that night? She lived down the street from the child, and while they weren't friends, they weren't enemies either. On a Friday night, in their second year of middle school, the girl had a slumber party, inviting all five of the child's only friends, but not the child. As if being left out weren't enough of an indignity, the girls toilet-papered and egged the child's house. The child pretended not to care, but was deeply hurt—more by the exclusion than the act of vandalism. At the urging of the girl's parents, the girl apologized to the child for the act of malicious mischief, swearing on her goldfish's life that it was done without malice. But she didn't explain why the child was barred from the party. In fact, she didn't even mention it. The child grudgingly forgave the girl and they never spoke of it again.

PSI-CHOSIS

Doctor Hauer was recommended by a member of the Alien's chess club. The intrusive thoughts and feelings had become overpowering. The Alien was one step away from committing what Earthlings referred to as Mass Murder. Adapting to their planet was proving to be far more difficult than It had ever imagined. The physical challenges were expected, but the mental and emotional had come as a complete surprise.

Upon entering the office, the Alien was greeted by the receptionist's pedestrian words delivered through a painfully artificial smile. "Good morning! May I help you?" is what she said, when she really meant: "Christ, I hate my fucking life! I'm old and fat, my son of a bitch husband is cheating on me, my ungrateful kids don't need me anymore, and my mind-numbing job makes me want to slash my fucking wrists!"

The telepathy was a significant part of the problem. Earthlings were seriously dysfunctional and tormented creatures, drowning in discontent and regret. Being subjected to their dissonant inner chatter for months on end was taking its toll on the Alien's equilibrium. It was like being on the receiving end of a miserable polycephalic organism's misplaced negative emotions. The Alien tried desperately to tune out the constant barrage of white noise, but Its brain had other plans.

"Would you sign in here, please?" the receptionist said, struggling to maintain her forced smile. Instead, the Alien heard her scream: "If I have to say *'Would you sign in here, please?'* one more fucking time I'm going to kill everyone in this goddamn office!"

After signing in, the Alien sat down and stared at the pabulumzines stacked on the table in front of It. Those insipid rags never failed to remind It of how out of place It was. It didn't care about fashion, celebrities, gossip... any of it. Averting Its gaze, It began surveying the room. The champagne carpet was filthy, the faux wood panel wallpaper was covered in dust and corner cobwebs, while the ceiling panels were held together with frayed duct tape. It wondered when the place had last been cleaned.

A sour and haggard looking nurse flung open the waiting room door, pointed at the Alien and growled, "You're up! Let's go!" Again, the Alien heard her true thoughts: "Oh, Dear God, the emptiness is worse than death. I'm so tired of being alone and having no one to share my life with."

The Alien let out a resigned sigh, then followed the nurse down the hallway to a cubicle-sized examination room that was in worse shape than the waiting room. It wondered why Its chess club acquaintance would have referred It to such an impersonal dump, but then remembered that Dr. Hauer was the only physician in the Alien's district who would provide free treatment.

Earthlings were required by law to be enrolled in the universal government's health insurance program, but since the Alien was an alien – in more than one sense of the word – It was unable to obtain benefits.

As the Alien propped Itself up on the examination table, the doctor came flying in. "Hello," he said in a monotone voice, robotically extending his hand, "I am Dr. Hauer. What can I do for you today?"

For some inexplicable reason, the Alien couldn't hear his thoughts, only the actual words coming out of his mouth. *How strange*, the Alien thought. Although thrown off, It was incredibly relieved to be speaking with someone who could help alleviate Its anguish. It wasted no time in explaining Its plight.

In response, the doctor planted his back against the wall, placed his thumb under his chin, and began regurgitating a torrent of jargon right out of a medical book, as if he were taking an oral exam. He rambled on for ten minutes, during which the Alien couldn't get a word in edgewise. Then, before It could ask a single question, the doctor shoved a token into Its hands and rushed out. "I will see you again in three weeks," he said, closing the door behind him.

Perplexed, the Alien wandered out to the waiting room, where the surly nurse was standing with a stack of files in her hand. "The vending machine's in there," she growled, pointing at an ominous crimson door that read PRESCRIPTIONS in large, white block lettering. The Alien hadn't noticed the door before. It was as if it had materialized while It was in with the doctor. "Stuff that token in the slot," the nurse continued, "and it'll cough up your drugs." What the Alien heard was most unsettling: "Another fresh zombie, coming right up!" *What did she mean by that?* It wondered, heading for the door. "Seymour Steinway!" the nurse yelled, her angry eyes darting around the room. "You're up!"

The following morning, after another restless night, the Alien ingested the first pill. According to the package insert, the medication would begin to take effect within an hour. The Alien felt anxious, but also hopeful that the alleged wonderdrug would eliminate or at least mitigate the debilitating state that had consumed It.

The Alien was on edge all day, but assumed it was psychosomatic, or perhaps a temporary side-effect of the potent medication. By evening, It was freezing and unusually wired. Its eyes felt strange as well, as though they were about to burst out of Its head. It went into the bathroom and looked in the mirror, only to find a pair of monstrously dilated pupils staring back at It. As It attempted to process the bizarre sight, a surge of galvanizing tension jolted Its body from head to toe, retreating as quickly as it had struck. *I hope that was merely a hiccup*, the Alien thought. It took a couple of deep breaths and splashed cold water on Its face, then wandered into the kitchen. Oddly, It had no appetite, despite the fact that It hadn't eaten since the previous evening. It poured some Cheerios and skim milk into a bowl, then grabbed a tablespoon from the silverware drawer and wandered into the den, ensconcing Itself in the leather recliner. The first bite tasted bland, with a bitter aftertaste. The Alien returned to the kitchen for a box of sugar, which It proceeded to pour all over the cereal. The next bite was better, but still difficult to get down. It forced Itself to eat the entire bowl, hoping the carbohydrates would function as a natural sedative, so It could get a restful night of sleep. Then, beyond Its control, It tore open the box of sugar and dumped a mountain of it onto Its tongue, allowing it to fully dissolve before swallowing. Before It knew it, It was shoving miniature candy bars into Its mouth by the handful. When those were gone, It inhaled the rest of the sugar, before moving on to the brown sugar, which It polished off within minutes. No matter how much sugary food It consumed, It couldn't satisfy Its sweet tooth. After devouring every speck It could find, It lay on the loveseat in the den and turned on the television. Shortly thereafter, It dozed off.

The Alien was jolted awake at 3:20AM and couldn't regain entry to Slumberland. The troubling symptoms from the previous night persisted throughout the day and into the evening. The Alien lumbered through the protracted hours, becoming increasingly disoriented as they oozed by. *Must be the usual side effects*, It thought. The drug had been approved, applauded, and touted by governmental health agencies across the globe, and prescribed to millions over the past five years, which meant it had to be safe... right?

On the third day, the Alien went to the megamall to pick up Its camera from the repair shop. It was the first time It had left the house in 41 hours, and by now, the pharmaceutical-induced malaise had hijacked Its vessel.

It felt as though It had floated out of Its body and was circling it, like a vulture flying around a fresh corpse. "Dissociation" was the first word that popped into Its mind. It had never experienced the phenomenon, but had read about it in a medical journal. Then there were the auditory hallucinations. Every sound that entered Its ears was saturated with a bewildering reverb effect. Worse yet, those distorted sounds were being heard at an ultra-intensified level. Being from another planet, the Alien already suffered from atmosphere-induced Hyperacusis, but it was now crushing.

The mall was oppressively crowded, like a raging river teeming with fish, endeavoring not only to swim upstream, but outswim each other in the process. The aggressive and competitive nature of their movement was distressing. While taking a moment to survey Its surroundings, the Alien noticed that the human(oid)'s faces were melting, stopping just short of losing their features altogether. Coupled with the garbled language cascading from their mouths, it was too much to bear. A rush of vertigo washed over the Alien, followed by a suffocative feeling, as though It were being smothered with a pile of warm bath towels. It could still breathe, but barely. It quickly sought refuge on a bench near the food court. Moments after sitting down, a family of five closed in. The toddler's wailing was deafening! The Alien screamed, *"Shut Up!!!!!"* then jumped to Its feet and walked as fast as It could toward the nearest exit. Within seconds, It was running. It was clearly in the throes of a full-blown panic attack. Again, It had never experienced a panic attack, but had read about it in that same medical journal. It felt as though It were racing up a down escalator and getting nowhere—the warped sounds and images worsening with each futile step. Through the grotesque haze, It spotted the glass doors leading to the parking lot. The nightmare was almost over... only 100 more feet to go... now 50... now 25... now 10... and *It was out... free*. It heaved an immeasurable sigh of relief, but was catapulted back into hysteria when It realized It couldn't remember where It had parked. Meandering through the packed lot, frantic and gasping for air, It was nearly on Its knees, crawling, when It spotted the tail end of Its car. It pounced on the passenger's side door, tore it open, threw Itself in, and slammed the door closed. It heaved another sigh of relief... then another... and one more. It was over... it was *finally* over. Or so It thought. A tingling sensation coursed through every nanometer of the Alien's body, before morphing into numbness accompanied by a prickly feeling, as though thousands of microscopic needles were being driven into Its skin. Then It realized It was paralyzed... Its entire body had fallen asleep. *Full-body Parethesia?* It thought. *Is that even possible?* It was indeed possible, and the Alien had no choice but to ride it out, hoping It could eventually move one of Its hands enough to grab Its phone and call for help.

Three unimaginably dreadful hours passed before the paralysis began to gradually lift, beginning with the fingers and toes. By then, the Alien had decided that calling for help wasn't such a wise idea after all. It would only bring unwanted attention, and the Alien needed to remain under the radar of The Powers That Be. As soon as It regained full motion, It drove home and locked Itself away in Its bedroom.

Twenty-three hours later, the Alien was back at Dr. Hauer's office, sitting in the cubicle-sized examination room, hoping for an explanation. Instead, it was the same drill, different pill. Strangely, the doctor wasn't at all surprised by the Alien's horrific experience with the medication. "Oh, sometimes that happens," he said in his characteristic monotone voice. The Alien wished It could read his true thoughts, but the doctor seemed to possess a mental force field. The Alien took his sketchy word that the adverse reaction was just an unfortunate fluke, and that the new medication wouldn't have the same effects. After acquiring Its prescription from the vending machine, like a bag of Peanut Butter M&Ms®, It headed home. Still plagued by uncertainty and fear, It decided to wait until the following morning to take the first pill.

For the next 19 days, the Alien ingested the tiny capsule at 10AM, and waited patiently for the drug to work the magic it had promised. Although there were no discernible changes, the Alien was beyond relieved that there wasn't a repeat performance of the previous nightmare. Until the 20th day, that is...

The Alien was in line at a convenience store, when It was tackled by the thoughts of everyone in the room, even though none of them were speaking, which had always been a requirement of the telepathy. *Never* had the Alien been able to hear a single thought unless the person was speaking words that usually contradicted what they were truly thinking. Then it happened again: that prickly sensation coursed throughout Its body and It was paralyzed on the spot. All It could do was stand there, motionless, drowning in the hideous streams of thought of the miserable creatures surrounding It.

"Man, I tell ya, if I could get away with it, I'd wrap my clammy hands around that rat bastard Semesky's neck and choke the goddamn life outta him!" From the mind of the construction worker standing directly in front of the Alien.

"Blondes are such stupid fucking sluts! God, I hate them!" From the mind of the pudgy brunette woman in front of the construction worker.

"What the fuck? The fat bitch behind me is getting way too close! Back the fuck off already, Bitch!" From the mind of the anorexic blonde woman in front of the brunette.

The turbaned Indian standing directly behind the Alien muttered some angry thoughts in Punjabi about how long it was taking, while the bald Caucasian man standing behind the Indian man ejaculated a mindful of racist thoughts about the Indian man.

It was Hell on Planet Earth, made more hellish by the inability to flee. Trapped, The Alien closed Its eyes, while concentrating with all Its might on moving Its hands over Its ears. Miraculously, the hands moved, and moments after shutting out the babel, It regained full motion of the rest of Its body. Terrified that the paralysis would return, It fled to the safety of Its car and then home.

There would not be another visit to Dr. Hauer's squalid office and his insidious vending machine that promised salvation and delivered terror. Unfortunately, the so-called panaceas had caused irreparable damage, and for the next several years, the Alien battled Demons far more formidable than It had ever encountered prior to seeking the gonzo physician's help. The problems It *thought* It was experiencing were a joke compared to Its current state. It struggled to survive in an atmosphere of unrelenting madness, until the day came when It could no longer cope. There were only two options: It could leave Earth and return home or end Its own life. That was it.

Or… *maybe Mass Murder was the solution after all?*

PATHOLOGICALLY OUTRAGED

Two creatures, presumed to be human beings, are sitting in a vivarium on opposite sides of a tinted glass dividing wall. One is male, the other female. It's unknown to the observers which is which. The creatures know they're there for a specific reason, but neither seems to know why the other is there. The observers have no idea why anyone is there, including them. After engaging in small talk for 14 minutes, the conversation between the two creatures takes a more purposeful turn.

SPECIMEN A: What are your thoughts on aging?

SPECIMEN B: I'm one of those people who criticize others for getting old... *and* for getting plastic surgery to look younger.

SPECIMEN A: Forgive my forwardness, but are those your real lips?

SPECIMEN B: Are you insane? Of course not!

SPECIMEN A: How about your political views? I don't mean, are they real, but rather, what are they?

SPECIMEN B: I'm one of those people with a smug sense of moral superiority... even though I consider myself broadminded.

SPECIMEN A: And how does that work for you?

SPECIMEN B: Beautifully, since most people think my views epitomize what it means to be broadminded, making my glaring hypocrisy inconsequential.

SPECIMEN A: Do you believe experience should play a role when forming opinions?

SPECIMEN B: I don't see why. I'm perfectly content sounding off like an expert on everything from Baby Cage Fighting to Intermittent Amnestic Anticipation Dysfunction With Glossolalia & Acute Rhinotillexomania Disorder[1]. What about you? How do you go through life?

SPECIMEN A: I'm one of those people who checks to see if the stove burner is on by placing my hand directly on it while asking, *Is this on?*

---

[1] Intermittent Amnestic Anticipation Dysfunction With Glossolalia & Acute Rhinotillexomania Disorder (IAADWGARD) is a psychical condition that involves unpredictable episodes of an aberrant inability to remember significant events or facts, worsened by the fear of it occurring, complicated by an uncontrollable urge to speak rapidly and loudly in an unintelligible language while picking the nose.

SPECIMEN B: I don't get it, which means I'm going to pass judgment on *it* and *you*.

SPECIMEN A: I think I may already know the answer, but what are your thoughts on capital punishment?

SPECIMEN B: I'll probably change my mind if it ever becomes popular to think otherwise, but as of right now, I vehemently oppose it... on the grounds that it's inhumane. I'm a card-carrying pacifist. Anyone who disagrees with my religious and political views should die the worst possible death, though. Especially the talking heads, pundits, and others who have no part whatsoever in the policymaking.

SPECIMEN A: Wouldn't it be more sensible, not to mention *humane*, to simply ignore the talking heads, pundits, and others who have no part whatsoever in the policymaking? Your anger toward them is futile, and they only thrive on it.

SPECIMEN B: *Ignore them?* Have you completely lost your mind? Then I would be stuck with several more hours a day that could be spent more productively and pleasurably.

SPECIMEN A: And what do you do for pleasure?

SPECIMEN B: I really get off on being outraged... or, at least, appearing to be outraged... and only on social media.

SPECIMEN A: I'm not sure I understand… can you elaborate?

SPECIMEN B: I spend several hours a day scouring the internet for issues to be outraged about. Then I post a flood of links to my DisplacementBook profile, without verifying their veracity. In fact, I don't even read, listen to, or watch any of the content… neither do any of the people who comment on my posts. Only the headline, thumbnail, and my clever caption matter.

SPECIMEN A: Outrage is a natural human emotion. It can be healthy and help bring about positive changes, although I think if someone were genuinely outraged about any given wrong in the world, that outrage wouldn't be limited to sounding off in the bubble of social media. Nor would it fade when that wrong's popularity fades in the bubble of social media, as is often the case.

SPECIMEN B: Who said my outrage was genuine? I have no idea what I think or feel about any of the crap I post. I just jump on the bandwagon with whatever hot issues are trending at the time, without doing a shred of research. I have no personal experience with the issues either. I only know that it feels orgasmic to vent my unflagging outrage to a captive audience. It's how I've defined myself on DisplacementBook… and I've amassed a sizable bunch of groupies to boot. They really think I'm a legitimate activist who's making the world a better place. Plus, they never notice that I'm constantly flip-flopping, fumbling, and contradicting myself while trying to figure out what I'm supposed to think.

SPECIMEN A: Are you familiar with a psychological condition called Pathological Outrage?

SPECIMEN B: I won't admit I'm not, since that would mean I'm not omniscient, so I'll just say *probably*.

SPECIMEN A: It's an addiction to the rush that comes from being or appearing to be outraged, complicated by a compulsion to show others that one is a righteous and enlightened being. Sufferers obsessively seek out issues about to be outraged about – often creating and ascribing their own subtexts – and then spew a torrent of posts onto social media sites, regardless of whether their sources are accurate, reliable, or current. Most curiously, sufferers rarely, if ever, take their outrage beyond the bubble of social media.

SPECIMEN B: That sounds like certain people in my DisplacementBook news feed.

SPECIMEN A: Well, it's an equal opportunity disorder, although sufferers erroneously believe that the only sufferers are people with views opposite to theirs. As with other addictions, denial runs deep.

SPECIMEN B: That sounds like certain people in my DisplacementBook news feed.

SPECIMEN A: It's becoming increasingly prevalent. Often mistaken for an online shtick by non-sufferers, the majority of sufferers are entirely unaware of their behavior or that they have a serious disorder. In its most critical stages, sufferers reach a point where they *want* horrible shit to happen in the world, so they can feed their habit more frequently.

SPECIMEN B: That sounds really unhealthy. I'm glad I don't fit the description.

SPECIMEN A: It is really unhealthy. When someone is chronically outraged, to a pathological and masturbatory degree, it's not only toxic, but also counterproductive. If *everything* is outrageous then nothing is.

SPECIMEN B: I wonder how much longer we're going to be here. I can't stand being away from my computer and phone for more than ten minutes. I'm beginning to feel anxious and sick to my stomach. In the time I've been sitting here, the whole world's probably gone to the dogs and I'm missing the show. My groupies must be experiencing withdrawal as well. By now, I would have posted at least a hundred links and memes.

SPECIMEN A: Do you ever feel inspired to find causes you truly feel passionate about, and then do what you can to make a real difference in the world?

SPECIMEN B: I wouldn't even consider it. That would require me venturing beyond the cozy confines of my computer and middle-class enclave, which would be uncomfortable and possibly dangerous. Why on earth would I ever do that? It's much safer, easier, and more rewarding for my ego to spout on the internet about the world's wrongs than to help remedy them. Let's face it... it's hell out there, and I have no interest in experiencing any of it first-hand. I mean, I've never visited any war-torn or poverty-stricken places... or spent more than five minutes in a ghetto, for that matter... and always while in motion, driving through as quickly as I can, with the doors locked and windows rolled up.

SPECIMEN A: I respect you for admitting it, at least. A lot of people wouldn't.

SPECIMEN B: I would never on DisplacementBook. The admirable reputation I've carefully contrived for myself would be destroyed, and my groupies would be devastated. Even though I rely largely on the words of others to express myself, they hang on it all, as if the words were my own. They also love my embellished posts about the good deeds I do for others, which are just basic courtesies most people would do without thinking and would never post about on the internet.

SPECIMEN A: Posting about the deeds does give the impression that you're more concerned with *showing* you're a good person, rather than simply being a good person, which, in a way, tarnishes the goodness of the deeds.

SPECIMEN B: What's the point of doing a good deed if you don't tell everyone and their grandma about it?

SPECIMEN A: Out of curiosity, what happens when your DisplacementBook friends express views contrary to yours?

SPECIMEN B: I post an infantile and histrionic tirade, demanding that they unfriend me immediately if they don't agree with *everything* I have to say.

SPECIMEN A: Wouldn't it be easier and more logical to just *unfriend them*? Or better yet, respect their rights to freedom of thought and expression? I thought you considered yourself broadminded?

SPECIMEN B: Unfriending them would be unwise. I would be failing to capitalize on a prime opportunity to throw an epic hissy fit that would not only garner volumes of attention, but also make my friends shake in their boots. It's intoxicating to wield that kind of power over people, especially people who don't know me outside of DisplacementBook.

SPECIMEN A: Doesn't that all sound unreasonable and somewhat tyrannical to you?

SPECIMEN B: *Absolutely not!*

SPECIMEN A: What else do you do for kicks?

SPECIMEN B: When I'm not busy being outraged, I get off on accusing younger creative people of being influenced by or outright copying creative people from my generation, which everyone knows is the greatest, most important, and most innovative generation in the history of mankind. It doesn't matter that the younger creative people can't help when they were born, or that they might be completely unfamiliar with the creative people I'm accusing them of being influenced by or outright copying. I'm resentful that they're younger, and feel entitled to misplace my ill feelings onto them with my baseless misassumptions.

SPECIMEN A: Does it make you feel better?

SPECIMEN B: Not really... but admitting that would mean I'm wrong.

SPECIMEN A: Then why do you do it?

SPECIMEN B: Because I'm supposed to, that's why! Jeez, you're really out of touch, aren't you? More than anyone I've ever met. Now, my *favorite* pastime is to gripe whenever I can, about whatever I can, no matter how insignificant it is... especially crap I can't change and crap that has no adverse effect on anyone. I mean, *everyone* enjoys doing that. Don't you?

SPECIMEN A: No. I find it pointless and poisonous, and it fills me with self-loathing. That doesn't make it wrong, though.

SPECIMEN B: *Really?* There must be something wrong with you then. You ought to seek help for that.

SPECIMEN A: Realizing and accepting that life is never going to stop flinging shit at me or anyone else makes it much easier to cope with whatever shit is thrown my way. It also helps me put said shit into perspective, and helps suppress the urge to kvetch about insignificant-in-the-grand-scheme shit. Above all, it helps me focus on and truly appreciate all that isn't shit, which accounts for better part. Although cynics would disagree, the world is as beautiful as it is ugly, if not more so. All you have to do is open your eyes and *choose* to see it for what it truly is.

SPECIMEN B: You're clearly delusional. The world is far, far worse than it's *ever* been. That's a fact.

SPECIMEN A: That is, in fact, an opinion. The copious availability of information combined with the media's inveterate and sadistic need to spotlight the negative only makes it *seem* as though the world is worse than it's ever been. The truth is, most of our present-day problems are merely relative and in some cases unique to our particular time.

SPECIMEN B: That's fine and dandy, but I have no real problems to speak of, which is why I thoroughly enjoy griping about whatever I can, and obsessing over the world's ugliness. It makes my trouble-free life seem far more interesting. You see, I'm relatively healthy, my marriage is happy, I have a beautiful home, I don't have to worry about money, I don't have to work at a job I hate, or at *any* job for that matter. I'm getting long in the tooth, which I'm not too pleased about, but it's not as if I can change that.

SPECIMEN A: What if you could?

SPECIMEN B: What do you mean?

SPECIMEN A: What if you could turn back the clock? Would you be willing to do whatever it takes?

SPECIMEN B: That depends on *whatever it takes* entails.

SPECIMEN A: What if, by promising to never gripe about petty crap ever again, you could have back every moment of your life that was spent griping about petty crap?

SPECIMEN B: Hell, that would buy me back at least twenty years. I could go for that, big time. What's the catch?

SPECIMEN A: If you gripe about petty crap *ever again*, *even once*, you'll drop dead right on the spot.

SPECIMEN B: Get out of here! That's ridiculous! You have a sick sense of humor.

SPECIMEN A: Who said I was kidding?

SPECIMEN B: Of course you're kidding!

SPECIMEN A: What if I'm not? What if I told you I had the power to make it happen? Do you think you could meet your end of the bargain?

Well, can you?

Apophenia is an imprint of paraphiliamagazine.com

For information and to purchase other titles:
paraphiliamagazine.com/books.html

www.ingramcontent.com/pod-product-compliance
Lightning Source LLC
Chambersburg PA
CBHW072241190626
46809CB00018B/2948